SPELLBOUND

JULIA GOLDHIRSH

PROLOGUE

Rose wandered through the forest beyond the city limits where she was raised. As she searched her surroundings, cold darkness coiled around her leg. It slithered like a slimy snake, clamping around her ankles. Panic clawed up her throat as she disappeared into the gripping darkness. Rose broke out of the void, darting towards an unknown destination on the eastern side of the forest. She was drawn to a river—why there, she didn't know.

At the foot of the river, Nightshade stood staring at Rose, his eyes like pits. He was frigidly animated. His pale, translucent skin radiated a threatening frost, and his hair was so dark it seemed to suck the light from his surroundings. The pointed teeth in his mouth were bone white, and when he spoke to her he seemed to chomp on the words in anticipation of trying to devour her existence.

"I couldn't manage to kill her, but I will kill you. Only one of Nymph blood can destroy my mirror!"

CHAPTER 1

Rose's eyes popped open, and she bolted upright in her bed, startled awake from her most recent nightmare. In an attempt to shake off any remnants of the icy image and threatening figure, Rose got out of bed to stretch her legs. Though she couldn't recall all of the details from her dream, she still found herself searching the corners of her room, seeking anything that might be lurking. Her gaze landed on the calendar hanging on the wall. She could hardly believe her birthday was only days away. Not just any birthday, but her sixteenth. It was time for a change.

In previous years, she'd asked for gardening supplies. But this year she'd grown tired of being the sole caretaker for this greenhouse. This year she wanted her freedom. That was a wish she doubted would be granted.

Rose peered through the clear glass of the greenhouse and saw her mother approaching from their cozy farmhouse, mere feet away. In the distance, she could see her father working the farmland as the sun rose, and she scrunched her nose and shuddered at the sight of him before turning her attention back to her mother's form. In every direction, she could see nothing but expanses of farmland. The only sign of civilization was the courier that visited once every few months. This only fed her hatred for this place.

Rose kicked a watering can in frustration then composed her face into a fake grin as her mother entered the greenhouse. As soon as her mother crossed the threshold, she began her usual chattering, causing Rose to roll her eyes in irritation. Rose allowed her mind to wander to self-destructive thoughts.

Why is she allowed to live freely? Why her and not me?

She clasped her garden shovel firmly and chided herself for the stray thought that crossed her mind. Hurting her to get away was not a good solution. She would *not* resort to violence *no matter* how irked she felt. She wasn't her father.

"Rose, are you well? Do you need me to bring you anything?" her mother crooned.

"Yes, mother, I'm fine." Rose gritted her teeth and feigned a smile.

Biting her lip to keep from screaming, she allowed her mother to launch into her daily line of questioning. Which began with the obligatory pleasantry of, "How are you?"

Of course, the only response allowed was, "I'm fine."

Rose tried to listen, but her consciousness slithered back to her sinister inner thoughts. Her typical, curt replies flowed from her mouth without much effort. It was a dance she did with her mother daily. Meanwhile, Rose entertained various scenarios of how she might express her frustrations to her mother. The one that she kept returning to would surely land her in jail. Hitting her mother over the head with a shovel would be momentarily satisfying, but jail was bound to be an even worse prison. Rose wasn't about to go there to suffer and die. Exchanging one cage for another wasn't appealing. Some part of her still held onto the bright hope of escape.

With a shake of her head, Rose tried to stave off her rage.

She just barely caught the end of her mother's speech, "…if you need anything, just let me know, and I'll get it for you."

Rose mumbled out, "I'm fine, mother!" and punctuated the sentence with her trademark eye roll.

Inhaling deeply, Rose forced her mind back to what she desperately wanted to ask about: *escape*—a relief from constant imprisonment because she couldn't take it anymore!

As she opened her mouth to boldly release her desires out into the open, she stumbled on her words and all that came out was "Now that I've become stronger… maybe I can leave this greenhouse… even if it's just for a little while."

Crimson bloomed on her mother's face and her head snapped around so fast the swish of her hair could've chopped down a tree. A grimace spread across her lips. Her eyebrows were pushed together in a scowl.

"But you are *bound* here! Do you wish to die, Rose? Leaving the greenhouse would be absolutely mad! Why would you want to leave now? You're still so young."

Rose whirled toward her mother and screamed, "I'm tired of being trapped here, Lailah. I want to explore the world. I've *always* wanted to leave. I never told you because I knew my staying here made you happy, but I can't take it anymore."

Having the audacity to use her mother's first name only added to her mother's anger. Lailah rushed out of the greenhouse so quickly that one of the pins holding her hair in its hastily constructed bun fell to the floor. As Lailah slammed the door closed behind her and locked it, Rose could have sworn she saw her mother smirk for the first time in ten years. This only made Rose more determined to leave. She began plotting her escape.

CHAPTER 2

That night, Rose used the hairpin which had fallen from her mother's hair to painstakingly pick the lock. Triumphantly, she sighed when the lock gave way. Quietly, she closed the door behind her and snuck out of the greenhouse under the cover of night.

That first breath of crisp air and the feeling of the night breeze on her skin made her head spin in delight. Pure joy engulfed her. She reveled in the glory of the ground beneath her feet and bathed in the moon's silvery glow. No glass obscured its brilliant light tonight. Gazing around in wonder, she now understood she'd rather die than continue living her life as an observer. Creeping over to the entrance, she risked a single, swift glance towards the entrance of the house. The lights were all off, and she breathed a sigh of relief.

Rose had to put distance between herself and the greenhouse quickly or else her mother would capture her and hold her in captivity once again. Being at the mercy of her fiend of a father was not Rose's top priority. The young woman wandered on until the heaviness of sleep curled around her bones. Then she rested on the hard ground, planning to continue her journey in the morning.

The warmth of the sun shining on her face woke her. Languidly, she stretched her limbs. They were slightly stiff and crackled as she stirred. The claws of sleep still clung to her even though she'd slept until mid-day.

Rose brushed off the exhaustion which seemed to come from her makeshift sleeping quarters, the ground, and continued on her adventure. She noticed when she looked behind her that her house was no longer in view. At first, there was only farmland and forest in her path, but after walking on for several miles, she started to see the outlines of what looked like a city. That vague outline urged her forward until she reached the village.

Stepping foot into her first-ever village was better than any picture her imagination could conjure up and more vivid and lively than the descriptions in all the books that she'd read, combined. The houses were crowded together like many flat-topped mountains. Gas street lights dotted the city like fireflies, though none of them were lit in the bright sunlight.

With excited steps, she strolled towards the town, feeling triumphant and successful in her escape. She had just crossed over the threshold into town when she collapsed to the ground in a coughing fit.

Victory crumbled before her as her knees slammed into the rocky, dirt street and her lungs heaved the air in and out of her body. Her knees tore open where she hit the ground. She began to cough up blood, staining the ground an inky crimson red.

All she could think was, *Why didn't I believe her?* as her dinner from the night before made a second appearance, splattering onto the street. Her hands trembling in pain and her violent coughing was the villager's first impression of her. She looked up, blood still running down her mouth.

The violent pain racking her body momentarily subsided as she gazed up at the handsome savior before her. It was a simple villager, a man. He spotted her pathetic retching form and lifted her into his mail carrier. Rose only managed to catch a glimpse of her protector before her vision went black.

When she came to, she felt the ground moving beneath her. She was in was a buggy, a small one for carrying mail. Every so often, they stopped and she saw him grasp letters from where she was resting. For a while, Rose simply took in the image of the man who had saved her. From behind him, all she could see was jagged, short, golden-brown hair and olive skin.

He seemed to sense her stir, then, and he turned around and said, "I was starting to wonder if you'd awaken. Are you feeling better?" She opened her mouth to say yes, but her chest constricted and her breathing was heavy. Her gaze darted around, looking for her greenhouse, the only thing that could save her.

"No. I need to get back to my house. I'm past the town just a few miles down the road," Rose gasped. She gave him some directions, vague ones, but he smiled with recognition and pointed his horse in the right direction.

"I'll take you there. You're in no condition to travel," the villager said. As Rose opened her mouth to gripe, she was stopped by the strange man's input. "No buts. Do you want to get yourself killed?" he said as his lips curled upward in a smile. His eyes glinted with wit.

"Fine," Rose huffed and pouted her lower lip in childish protest.

A bright smile graced his face and humor danced across the emerald green of his eyes in response. He turned back around to direct the horse towards her village.

Her chest heaved and another coughing spell ripped through her. Thankfully, she placed her hands in front of her mouth just in time to catch the blood in her palms. Black spots danced in front of her vision, and Rose fought to keep a hold of consciousness as they traveled back to her home.

By the time they finally reached her house, her bones rattled and her chest felt as though it were filling up with water. She was becoming worse with every passing minute. Her clothes were stained the same red-black color as her hair.

Rose rasped to the concerned face of the villager, "I must return to the greenhouse now."

He looked to the greenhouse, the main house, then back at her. "Wouldn't you be safer in the house—?"

Rose cut him off and snapped, "No, I wouldn't. If you won't take me to the greenhouse, I'll walk there myself."

Pushing herself to her feet and trying to force her way to the greenhouse proved impossible when her knees buckled beneath her. She collapsed to the ground, barely breaking the fall with her palms before her arms folded like paper doll arms.

Inching her way towards the greenhouse brought to her mind the irony that she was now crawling towards the very place she had tried to escape the night before. As she reached for the greenhouse, strong arms grasped her waist and lifted her off the ground as if she were as light as a feather.

Rose looked up to see the strange man, and was surprised at how he'd lifted her with such ease. He carried her to the glass house as carefully as if she were a small child, though, to Rose, his lack of facial hair and softer features suggested that he was little more than a child himself.

As soon as they entered the greenhouse, Rose was finally able to guzzle in air. When she inhaled, it didn't inflame her throat and the lead weight on her chest lightened slightly. Her exhales weren't wet with blood. Each lungful of air came a little easier, but she still wasn't fully recovered. The vice still gripped her chest—not squeezing the life out of her anymore, but squeezing nonetheless. "Can you take me closer to the roses?" Rose asked, nodding her head in the direction of the white roses.

He shifted her in his arms and then started striding towards the roses. As she got closer, her breathing steadied, the urge to cough subsided, and the pain in her lungs dissipated.

By the time they had reached the roses, the only part of her that wasn't healed were her hands. The hands were still numb and the fingers moved clumsily from stiffness.

"Can you put me down? I want to try to walk now," Rose asked the man, and he placed her gently on the ground.

As she sat on the floor amidst the fragrant blossoms, she reached a trembling hand out to stroke the rose's velvety petals. Miraculously, the feeling began to return to her hand. She cupped one of the blossoms with both her hands. For a moment, she just stared at the flowers in awe as she felt them heal her ragged and broken body. Rose thought, *It isn't the greenhouse that keeps me here after all. It's the plants. Maybe escape is still an option.*

Rose pushed herself from the ground, only wobbling slightly before she managed to find her balance.

She looked the villager in the eyes and said, "Thank you for helping me." She realized she'd never even asked this man's name or introduced herself. "My name is Rose. What would your name be?"

"Gabriel," he said.

As Rose stared at her clumsy, bloodied hands, a memory of her childhood flashed before her mind.

CHAPTER 3

Rose was eight years old. The sky was painted a vivid midnight blue and the stars graced it with their silvery glow, dotting the sky by the millions. While all the cockerels, cows, other children, and even the flowers seemed to sleep, Rose lay wide awake. The brightness of the moon and the beauty of the midnight sky beckoned her awake. She was restless, hungry for food and some adventure. She reached beneath her pillow, a favorite hiding spot, and pulled out a thin wire coat hanger that she'd fashioned into a lock pick some time ago. Sneaking out of the greenhouse for a midnight snack was one of her favorite past times.

As she tiptoed on quiet feet, trained through years of practice, Rose shimmied the lock with practiced hands, and it swiftly clicked open. She poked her head out of the greenhouse, her curtain of red-black hair swaying as she looked left and then right before slinking towards the house. Pressing her back against the greenhouse wall, she moved quietly against the cool glass wall of the conservatory until she reached the front door of her parent's abode.

When she got to the door, she took some salt and beef tallow from her dinner to grease the door lock and handle then slid her makeshift lock pick in. A faint click cued her to painstakingly twist the handle. Thankfully, it didn't squeak.

Rose peeked her head in, searching first the stairs then the hallway for her parents, but saw nothing. Slowly sneaking through the hallways, she headed towards the pantry and grabbed some of her favorite snacks. As she was leaving, she overheard talking. Despite knowing that she should turn back, her curiosity got the best of her, and she crept towards the sound. She edged around corners until she saw them. Mother's hair was mussed and father's eyes were bloodshot. He swayed on his feet. Her mother and father were talking.

"Why did you have to make that deal? Now, we're stuck with her," lamented her father.

Tears welled up in her mother's eyes. "I thought this was what you wanted. We prayed for a child for so long," she said with her voice breaking.

"I didn't want this *thing*, a burden of a child who can't even leave the greenhouse. We can't marry her off either," he said with a grimace. His nose scrunched up in distaste.

"How dare you insult our only daughter like that!" she said, her voice rising to a scream.

"She's no daughter of mine. She's a daughter of that wench of a Nymph!"

A gasp escaped Rose's lips. She covered her mouth trying to muffle the sound, but she already felt his dark gaze swivel towards her. With a stride that betrayed his impaired state, he quickly rushed over to her.

When he saw the wire lock pick, he struck her face with the thin metal, quick as a whip. His breath smelled of salve. The brute loomed over her. "What's wrong with you? Do you have a death wish sneaking in here?" He leaned over to hit Rose once more, but Lailah grabbed him to try to stop the strike.

"Rose are you okay?" her mother asked. "She was just trying to get a snack. Leave her be!" Lailah shouted.

At that, he turned his hatred-filled gaze towards Lailah.

He shouted at her, "Don't let that ungrateful brat have anything. I'll teach her what happens when you don't listen to your parents. Those with thieving hands will learn."

He rushed towards the gas stove and turned on the burner.

"No!" her mother shrieked. She tried to rush him, but he batted her away, and she fell to the floor.

He then took Rose's hand and shoved it into the fire. Her skin blistered and peeled. The scent of burning stung her nose and she screamed and bucked trying to get away, but it was no use.

Rose's mother charged after them. She rammed into him as hard as she could and threw him off balance. Rose took the chance to yank her hands from his and race off towards the greenhouse. It was too late, however. The damage was done.

☆ ☆ ☆

Rose shook her head bringing herself back into reality to see Gabriel looking directly into her eyes, but his mind was somewhere else judging from the blank stare plastered on his face. Now that he was standing in front of her, she noticed that his build was smaller than she'd originally thought. Even at his full height, he barely eclipsed her own meager stature. His skin was tanned and worn, clashing with his younger features.

CHAPTER 4

I have to help her, was the first thought that sprang to Gabriel's mind, though he had no idea why. She reminded him of someone, but he couldn't quite place the memory. Her curvaceous frame and the confident way she carried herself were familiar, but her chilling red eyes marked her as something strange, even otherworldly.

Gabriel saw Rose stare up at him with questioning eyes and realized he'd said his thoughts aloud. Blood rushed to his face in response, and he averted his gaze slightly.

"You're sick, but perhaps I can find someone who can cure you," Gabriel said.

He doubted he could help, but something familiar about Rose made Gabriel crave the chance to try. She reminded him of Lara despite their differing appearances, and he didn't want Rose to suffer that person's fate. The thought of her misery tugged at his heart.

He turned back towards her and saw doubt creep into her eyes. Gabriel reached out to touch Rose's cheek, but retracted his hand when her weary eyes met his.

Gabriel straightened his posture, attempting to regain some composure. "Just tell me how to help you and it's done," he said.

Rose's face was still set in a doubtful frown. The face of the person he'd once known flitted across Rose's features, and his need to help this woman flared brighter than before. A memory of Lara, her skin pale and her eyes closed, burned into his mind. Sick in bed, hoping for a cure that would never come.

"Can you teach me about the outside world?" Rose mumbled.

Gabriel was pulled back to the present by this strange request. Struck silent, he didn't understand her question.

How does she not know about the outside world? he thought.

His eyes scanned the interior of the greenhouse and landed on the makeshift house made of a small, wooden garden shed. Dry laundry hung on a clothesline strung to the side. Books and other personal items dotted the floor. Understanding dawned across his face. This place wasn't just used to grow food in winter. It was a house. She lived in here.

Does she ever leave the greenhouse? Gabriel thought.

The question must have been evident on his face because Rose said, "I live here."

"Why? What happened?"

"I live here. I've spent my whole life within these four glass walls with my mother as my jailer. She's done her best to make it livable, which is why you see the mock house and books strewn about. She's done her best to educate me on the world, and the rest I've learned from books that I taught myself to read."

Gabriel stared at her, trying to understand.

"She's always told me I was bound to here by a curse, but I never believed her until now." Rose thought for a moment, noticed Gabriel's reaction, then continued.

"I thought I was put here due to her being over-protective, to get me away from the dangerous, beastly man lurking in the house," she said, rolling up the sleeve of her blouse and revealing the discolored skin beneath. "The burns you see on my hands were from him."

Gabriel shuddered, looking at the scars.

"Now, I'm thinking there really is some form of curse keeping me here, but I have no information on its origin or on how to break it."

CHAPTER 5

After hearing her story, his brow creased with concern and his eyes were ablaze with intrigue. The first words out of Gabriel's mouth were, "What can I do to help?"

Her head cocked to one side as if expecting a punchline. When there was none, her eyes widened in surprise and confusion. "You…uh…you…want to…?"

Gabriel watched on with amusement, suppressing the smile that tried to spread across his face as he watched her fumble with her own words.

Rose turned away from him to toy with the petals of a nearby rose. He could hear her taking deep breaths in an attempt to compose herself. When she had finally calmed down, she turned back to him and said, "Have the doctors see if they can find out what's special about these roses. They seem to be my lifeline."

Gabriel searched her eyes to see if she was being serious. *She couldn't be serious, could she*, he thought to himself. Then, a quick survey of her solemn glance told him he was traveling into uncharted territory by helping Rose, and that these roses were his key into a new world.

He grabbed the roses from Rose and said, "I'll find a cure. I promise," before he set out on a journey that would change his life forever.

☆ ☆ ☆

The first place Gabriel thought to go was the local doctor. He rushed over and arrived in a flurry, hair mussed, and eyes ablaze with urgency. Upon his arrival, he presented the rose in question. The medic scrutinized the flower, but as he looked, his brow scrunched up and a puzzled look crossed his features. After what felt like an eternity, he simply shook his head and told Gabriel, "I can't do much without the patient here, but you can try to have a botanist help you. Maybe, it's a special species of plant."

Gabriel shifted on his feet. Nervous energy thrummed through him. "Please tell me where to find this botanist. It's urgent."

The doctor paused slightly and pursed his lips together before revealing the botanist's location. "He lives in a cottage attached to a greenhouse. It's on the outskirts of town and is overrun with strange plants. It's partially hidden by the dense forests. Be careful if you venture there. At night, strange things happen in those woods, and some of the townspeople have gone missing."

Gabriel gulped and scuffed his foot against the floor.

"Well then I better get going before the sun sets. Thank you," he said and he rode his horse and buggy to the cottage in the woods.

Chapter 6

Rose paced impatiently as she waited for Gabriel to return. Gabriel had left behind a remnant of the outside world, a note to her before he'd gone to find a cure.

Rose was beginning to get worried. *Where is he? He hasn't been back for almost a month now,* she thought to herself as she continued to pace and read the letter. She immediately halted her strides when her mother barged into the greenhouse. She'd come bearing gifts of eggs and milk, but her face contorted when she saw Rose holding a letter. She snatched the letter from Rose's hands and read it over. Her face flushed red and her hands tightened to a vice grip that slightly crumpled the letter.

"What is this?" Lailah said as she waved the letter in front of her face. "Have you been outside of the greenhouse," her mother asked. Barely concealed anger edged her tones.

Rose's gaze drifted to the floor to avoid her mother's disapproving glare, her silence a confirmation of her misdeeds.

"What were you thinking, Rose? You could've been killed. Do I have to start taking extra precautions to make sure you don't escape? Chains maybe? Do I have to live here with you like I did when you were a little girl?" Her voice was shrill now and rising to a screech.

"No, mothe—" Rose tried to say, but was cut off as her mother continued to talk over her.

"Yes that's exactly what I'll have to do from now on. I'm going to watch you until you truly learn how dangerous the outside world is for you," Lailah said, and then stormed off to get her possessions from the house.

At her mother's last statement, repressed terror filled her eyes. The sting of a metal wire and man with a devilish glint in his eyes darted across her thoughts. Just as her mother was leaving, Gabriel approached the greenhouse. This time, he wasn't wearing his traditional mischievous smile. His face was creased with worry.

He must have overheard the argument, Rose thought.

When Gabriel reached her, she knew she was right. The first words out of his mouth were, "We need to leave."

Rose yanked a few of the roses, roots and all, from the nearest bush then hurried after Gabriel. They got into the carriage and started riding away. As Gabriel and Rose took off, they saw Rose's mother walk out of the house. She caught sight of them, but she didn't yell, scream, or chase after them. Her face deflated with defeat and tears rolled down her cheek. An image of Rose pale, dead from the curse most likely flitted through her thoughts. Some combination of relief and sorrow overtook Lailah. She gazed solemnly at Rose and Gabriel's retreating form, looking as if her sole hope was that Rose would come back in one piece.

CHAPTER 7

When they got further away from the greenhouse, Gabriel slowed the carriage down. He looked over to Rose, who seemed perfectly healthy. Rose was looking at him with worried eyes, and he realized that she was scanning over his stitched up arm and his horse's scrapes and scratches.

"Are you well?" Gabriel asked.

"I should be asking you that. What happened to you?" Rose replied.

"I fell off my horse while I was on my way to the doctor's office looking for a cure." He faked an easy laugh, hoping she wouldn't notice the lie, not wanting to explain the lengths he'd gone to looking for medicine. Not just yet, anyway.

"That's what took you almost a month?" She raised an eyebrow at him questioningly, but didn't press further when he shrugged his shoulders in response.

Gabriel's focus went back to his concern for her. He was worried that, at any moment, Rose would collapse to the floor of the buggy and start coughing up blood, but to his surprise they made it back to his home without a hitch. Rose looked at him in surprise when they stopped in front of a cozy looking cottage. She gave Gabriel a questioning gaze.

"This is my home," Gabriel said.

"A home," Rose whispered to herself.

Gabriel smiled at her awestruck gaze.

Gabriel led Rose into the house and watched as she began to look around. She ran her fingers along the walls, painted dark green, like the vines of a flower. The gorgeous, dark wood glistened in the sunlight. Beautiful, cathedral windows graced the living room.

Rose perused through it like a breeze floating through his house, airing out the musty remnants of death that still clung to the house like a leech on skin. She skimmed over her surroundings, pausing only momentarily to take it all in, and then moving onto the next room. The dining room came next, and when she came across it, she paused. It was just a modest room with a small wooden table, simple lighting, and a couple of carved oak chairs. But, it wasn't the furniture that drew Rose in, it was the study just beyond. It was overflowing with books and called to her like a siren's song.

Bookshelves towered from floor to ceiling and stood proudly in this room. Despite all the books, there was not a speck of dust to be found. She guessed that a housekeeper had visited recently.

Gabriel watched as Rose scanned the bindings of the books with her fingertips, then paused on a book, and plucked it from its place on the shelf. She plopped down into a chair and began to read. He was interested in this side of Rose. She looked… content, just sitting at the dining room table reading. He wanted to let her enjoy her newfound freedom for a while, so he left his gift for her on the table, and walked outside to tend to the mail cart.

When Gabriel reached his buggy, he noticed that the roses were still resting, stems and all, on the floor. He tied his horse and buggy to the post in the back of the house, then he picked up the roses and grabbed some dirt which he hastily placed into a glass that was outside, collecting water. He waltzed back in and began planting the roses in small glasses and vases that he prepared with dirt and water. He placed a plant in each glass and placed the glasses around the house. He put one rose in each of his two bedrooms, one in the dining room, and one in the living room. His thoughts wandered back to the last stop he'd taken on his quest for a cure.

He had made it to the botanist's cottage just as the sun's rays were sinking below the skyline and painting the sky with glorious shades of orange and pink. The cottage was overgrown with weeds and vines. A small greenhouse stood in the back with plants growing all over the exterior walls. The only indicator someone still lived here was the light that was on the inside of the cottage. He tied his horse to the lone post several feet from the entrance of the cottage, slightly into the forest, then walked over to the door.

He knocked lightly and was startled by how suddenly the door swung open as if the man had been expecting him. The man was short, with thinning silver hair and wide brown eyes, but something about him felt off. His stride had the lithe and grace of a man many years his junior despite the cane he used as he strode along.

"What brings you to my cottage?" he croaked. "I haven't had a visitor since medicine started advancing. Herbalists like me have been deemed archaic, obsolete."

"Well, you see sir, I've run into a problem that today's medicine seems unable to solve. It has to do with these roses," Gabriel said and presented the white roses to the strange man.

Gabriel thought recognition flashed across the man's face at the sight of the roses, but it was gone too quickly to tell for sure. Wide-eyed, he turned back to Gabriel.

"Why are these roses so important?" he asked.

"Well, sir, I believe they may be the only cure for my friend. When she's away from the roses too long, she gets very sick and has trouble breathing. Can you help me?"

"How long has she been like this?" he asked.

"Her entire life. The doctors suspect bronchitis, but are unsure," Gabriel answered.

The man seemed to ponder what Gabriel said for a moment, then he snatched the roses and went over to the vials and poultices on his work table. He grabbed a pestle and mortar along with some vials and other various items including a strange porous cloth, a rainbow assortment of oils, and a chunk of wax. The man strode over to the connecting greenhouse and Gabriel followed along in awe of the contrast between this place and the doctor's office.

As Gabriel gazed around, he noticed there were several plants and herbs he could name plus a vast many more that appeared to be from another realm, plants with purple skins and covered in spiky thorns. Shelves filled with vials lined the walls, and it was difficult to tell where the greenhouse ended and the cottage began. Even the inside of the small abode was overrun with plants and vines that snaked the edges of walls and the underbellies of shelves.

The man grabbed some herbs and ground them up with a mortar and pestle then mixed in what looked like water. He poured it all into a vial and handed it to Gabriel.

"This will help with her symptoms, but I have some conditions for you using this medicine." A wicked grin spread across his face.

"What are they?" Gabriel leaned away from the man, shuddering at the darkness in his smile.

"First, you must never tell the girl where you received this medicine. I like my privacy. Second, I will not accept money for this medicine, but I will require a favor from you. No matter what favor I request you must agree. Do you understand?"

"Yes, but may I think about it?"

"You may take the medicine, but if you use it or destroy it in any way, I will expect my payment. If you cannot pay, then a great misfortune will fall upon you," He said that with what Gabriel thought looked like a sinister smile, but maybe it was just his imagination.

He left in the shroud of darkness, the warning the doctor had given him had slipped his mind. While exiting the cottage, he gazed up at the curtain of darkness dotted with stars and awareness dawned on him. Gabriel knew he needed to leave as soon as possible.

While fumbling blindly through the darkness, his horse began neighing and stomping its hooves. When he got closer, the golden eyes of wolves were glowing back at him. He had just enough time to grab a large stick from the ground before the wolves were upon him.

The wolf ran towards him, and he dropped to the ground to be on eye level with the wolves. One began to tear at his arm, and he shoved the stick into its eye. It howled in pain and loosened its grip. Another wolf tried to go for his throat, and he stuck the stick in its mouth then bashed its head with his fist as hard as he could and pushed it off him. He raced to his horse and hopped on. Hastily unchaining the spooked animal proved difficult, but after a couple of fumbled attempts, he unchained the horse and rode off into the night.

Only later would Gabriel notice that neither of them had gotten away unscathed. Shortly after making it to town, the horse's gait wavered and he jumped off. After quickly inspecting the animal, he noticed scratches and teeth marks trailing along its legs. He too was covered in claw marks and had a large gash with bite marks at its center, blood flowed freely from the wound. He knew that they would both need medical treatment before returning to the greenhouse.

Racing over to the doctor's office with the horse in tow was a challenge. Upon arrival, the doctor had been able to quickly take care of them both. He rattled off a list of questions including if his horse had been given a rabies vaccine and if he, himself, had been vaccinated.

He replied with, "I'm not sure. My wife always tended to the horse before she passed away. I think that I got the shot recently, but I don't remember."

"Okay. In that case, you both should get a full round of rabies shots. It will be a couple of weeks for us to do a full course of the vaccine. I will go fetch a veterinarian to treat the horse, and I'll stitch up your arm as well."

The doctor had left the room and rushed over to get help. He was able to get a veterinarian from a few buildings over to take a look at the horse while he treated Gabriel. After cleaning out his wound, the doctor painstakingly stitched up the gash and gave him a booster shot of the vaccine.

Time passed and when they had both healed, although both of them were still a little worse for wear, Gabriel set back off to meet Rose.

☆ ☆ ☆

Touching the medicine in his pocket brought him back to the present.

Gabriel knew taking the deal with the strange medicine man was too risky. The strange man had to be up to no good. If he used the medicine and didn't complete the favor, then a great misfortune would befall him.

But, what would happen if the worst option ended up being his only option?

When he was done placing the roses around the house, he walked into his bedroom and lowered himself onto his bed so he could get some sleep before the next mail delivery. Immediately, his thoughts drifted off and he fell into a restless slumber plagued with nightmares.

A haunting figure with a wicked grin appeared. A thick miasma formed around the figure. The man's hair was black as night, and his eyes were like lumps of charcoal. Soulless and lifeless.

Here's my request for you. I want Rose and Belladonna dead.

Gabriel's eyes popped open. Judging by the light in the sky, he would guess that it had been only about an hour since he'd tried to rest. He got up, and headed over to where he had left Rose reading. He would get Rose settled in before his next route.

CHAPTER 8

She was about a hundred pages into her book when she finally peeked up and noticed a crimson bag on the table wrapped in a red silk bow. Rose untied the ribbon and slid the silk off the mystery gift to reveal a hand held mirror set in silver. The silver lining had vines carved into it that reached toward the top of the mirror, and where the vines met, was a silver rose with its petals unfurled.

Just as she finished taking in the gift, Gabriel approached her and said, "You're welcome."

Rose whirled around. Gabriel was leaning in the doorway that separated the living and dining room. A sly toothy grin was up for display, but it was etched with a tired weariness. Rose wanted to say that Gabriel needed rest, but Gabriel kept her mouth shut with his quick input of "Now, let me show you to your room."

Gabriel began to lead Rose through the doorways of his house. Along the way she noticed beautiful paintings of rivers and forests decorated the hallways. The walls were painted in beautiful soft blues.

The parlor room was decorated with intricate vases of indigo that had handles of etched gold molded into the shape of dragons. Another vase was copper with a haphazard splotched pattern plus several more in shades of silver and one in crimson with an intricate designed that twisted and turned like snakes intertwined.

As they continued through the house, she caught a glimpse of a bathroom across the hall with a flushable toilet. Surprise was evident on her face. Those were expensive! Her home still only had chamber pots and a small tub.

After passing through a long hallway, they soon reached the bedrooms. Rose walked through the passageway of the first bedroom she saw and glanced around.

The room had the elegance of a woman's room, and contained the collections of a man's room. There was a half-finished needlepoint on the bedside table. The dressers were topped with creams, rouge, and blotting paper. A pocket watch and a razor laid next to the makeup. It seemed strange that such opposite personalities could mingle in one room. Rose's gawking abruptly ended when she heard, "This would be my bedroom." from Gabriel.

She'd stumbled upon something personal and the awkward situation caused laughter to bubble up from her throat. It sounded strange to her, airy and musical like wind chimes in a breeze. This caused Gabriel to also erupt in hysterics with her. It was as if her happiness were a butterfly he'd caught in his hand, which tickled at his skin with each light beat of its fragile wings.

Eventually, their spontaneous laughter subsided, and they gasped to fill their lungs with air. Gabriel led Rose over to the other room.

The rooms were polar opposites. Although this bedroom looked like it had recently been cleaned, it held few possessions. The room had a mostly Spartan setting.

There were two dresses trimmed with lace. One was the color of the sky on a cloudless day and the second was the color of a roaring fire. They were hanging in the closet near a full length mirror meant for a woman to gawk at her own beauty. She guessed that another woman had once lived here. The other items in the room were necessities, a small bed and a dresser.

Rose turned to ask Gabriel about the room, but noticed his eyes were shadowed and distant. The humorous Gabriel gave way to a somber side, but this Gabriel quickly disappeared.

Rose scrutinized Gabriel pasting on a smile, and forcing some humor into his voice. It grated on her nerves. The fake smile didn't fit him.

"This will be your room," Gabriel announced with a sweeping gesture.

Now that Rose had caught a glimpse of Gabriel's serious side, she had trouble seeing him as the happy person that his smiles and tone of voice were suggesting. Rose was having trouble picturing the carefree person Gabriel had always been during his visits. The forced lightness in his tone or the smile on his face could not erase the sternness from earlier. Gabriel frowned as he studied her. He knew he wasn't fooling her with his act. Sighing deeply, he spun on his heel and stalked toward the door. Just before he crossed the threshold, Rose whispered, "Thank you."

Gabriel's only acknowledgment of Rose's *thank you* was the corner of a sad smile that Rose managed to catch before he left her in her new room, alone.

CHAPTER 9

Eventually, Rose drifted into a fitful sleep. Voices nagged at her mind. They started out as a faint, ethereal humming and gradually rose to more distinct words. When she became able to hear the words, she was frightened by the echoing, otherworldly voice.

You can't leave me, my flower...

Come back to me, Rose, or else you will die.

Her greenhouse came into view. She was in the section normally filled with her roses. But now there was only one rose blooming. A red one.

There was a woman. Impossibly, she floated inches above the ground. Her skin was clad in leafy foliage. Before Rose's eyes, the red blossom bloomed then changed shape, slowly becoming a... human.

The rose was her.

All around, the garden began to wither and die. As the plants shriveled, Rose found herself growing ill. A tightness squeezed her lungs. She was fading, dying like the plants. She screamed out in pain as her chest tightened, shortening her breaths. The roses wilted, their stems bending, submitting to gravity. The leaves of plants crumpled up browning at the edges. She felt herself becoming ill with the flowers. The garden rotted before her eyes. Her lungs crushed her from the inside, collapsing in on themselves. She, too, was weakening. Rose wheezed and fought for air and a clamp grasped firmly on her heart.

Rose woke up screaming. She was coated in a cold sweat. "It was just a dream," Rose said to herself, but a nagging voice said, *"It was past, but it shall be again."*

At the words she began to shiver. Just then, Gabriel stormed into the room with mussed hair and his wild eyes darted around the room.

He was searching for signs of an intruder. When he found Rose alone, he approached her. Worry creased his brow.

Rose nearly jumped into the ceiling at the sudden sound of reality. She feared her dreams had entered her life.

Gabriel sat down on the edge of the bed, but made no immediate move to comfort her. He simply looked on at her then asked tentatively, "Are you well, Rose?"

"It was just a night terror, Gabriel. I'm well. You may rest now," Rose said, but hesitation laced her tone.

"If I may, I shall guard your bedside this night," Gabriel replied.

"If you wish, then you may," Rose said.

Gabriel walked from the room, and she feared he might not return, but a few moments later he brought in a chair from his living quarters. He pulled it so it was just beside the bed and carefully lowered himself into the seat.

"You may sleep now, Rose. I shall watch over you," Gabriel said and gave Rose his trademarked smile.

"I suppose this sleeping arrangement would be considered inappropriate to common folk, but I believe our circumstances make this situation justified," Rose said.

With that last sentence, Rose closed her eyes and fell back to sleep.

CHAPTER 10

Rose awoke to the warmth of sunlight beaming down on her face. She turned on her side to block out the sun that was streaming through the bare window. After a few moments of lying on her side, Rose realized she wasn't going to get anymore sleep, so she slowly slid out of bed and some of the covers fell to the floor in a heap, revealing the cotton dress she'd been wearing for the past couple of days.

Rose walked to the window and noticed a couple of roses standing in drinking glasses in the otherwise barren window sill. The petals were browning at the edges, and the stems slouched over like an old man with a cane. She ruffled the petals then headed towards the dining room led by the scent of bacon wafting through the air.

Rose entered the dining room, and when she didn't find the source of the smell, she continued on into the kitchen. There were a few cupboards filled with nonperishables. Next to one of the cupboards was a large icebox. Gabriel added some wood to the fire, then flipped the sizzling bacon in the aluminum frying pan. He continued to cook without taking any notice of her entrance into the kitchen.

He flipped the bacon effortlessly until it got perfectly crisp, and eventually, as if acting upon some invisible cue, Gabriel grabbed a bucket of water and dumped it on the fire dousing the flames. When he turned around he said to Rose, "Pardon me for not answering you upon your entrance, but cooking with this stove requires a watchful eye."

"That's okay. Th…thank you for last night" Rose stammered. Her cheeks flushed pink.

He ruffled his hair and an easy smile that made her heart flutter broke out on his face. "It wasn't any trouble. Everyone has nightmares sometimes, right? When I awoke a few hours before sunrise, I decided to cook breakfast. I made some for you as well."

He took the frying pan off the stove, and poured the contents onto two plates, then placed the plates on the dining room table. Gabriel pulled out one of the chairs and stood aside to give Rose room to sit.

"Please have a seat," Gabriel said.

"Thank you."

She tucked her dress beneath her and sat down in the chair. She sawed at the thick bacon with her knife, then speared it with her fork and shoveled it into her mouth. The taste was salty and much richer than her current fare. Although her food was fresh, Rose had never been a spectacular cook and relished the perfectly-cooked bacon and eggs. Holding the delicious flavors in her mouth a moment longer, savoring each morsel. Across the modestly sized table, Gabriel sat down and began to do the same, but at a much quicker pace. After he finished, he said, "I have business to attend to in the city. Afterwards I shall take you to the doctor, so he may see what causes your ailing."

Gabriel stood and left the dining room, and a few moments later, she heard the front door shut behind him. Rose proceeded to put the dishes on the countertop, since she wasn't sure where to wash them. She wondered if this doctor could really help with her strange illness. Apprehension gripped her, and she balled her hands into fists. Remaining hopeful but realistic would be the only way to make it through this.

She headed back towards the bedroom. Gabriel had let her sleep in, and she noticed in between the two bedrooms was another room. She opened the door and saw a metal tub and a flushing toilet. *It's the washing room from earlier*, Rose thought to herself, and made a mental note to wash up later.

Rose walked back into her room and began to look through the partially filled closet. Concern clouded her thoughts as she noticed all the women's clothing. She felt Gabriel's sadness toward the woman who must have previously owned these clothes, but the temptation to try them on was strong. She leafed through the few dresses in the closet and put on her favorite one.

It was a blue silk dress with a semi-circle of lace covering the top of her chest. Along the side of the blue silk were small red lines of satin.

The sleeves slid halfway along her arm and flared out slightly at the end. She inspected herself in the mirror, and was surprised that the dress fit her.

Rose quickly changed back into her cotton dress and hung the blue dress back up in the closet, and then collected what cleaning implements she could and said, "Time to start cleaning."

CHAPTER 11

Gabriel's job as a courier and part-time lamplighter had always been tiring, but today it seemed soul-draining. The pile of letters, packages, notes, and items for the hospital was like a bottomless well. No matter how many items he delivered, there was always more to be done. Today, as he gazed at what was left in his carriage, despair filled him. It felt like he wasn't even making a dent in his workload. Shaking his head, he grabbed the next load and trudged up the path to drop off the remaining mail. His heart was so heavy. Gabriel knew it had nothing to do with dropping things off at the hospital. The source of his distress was at home waiting for him. Trusting him to help her.

He needed to finish work early today, so he could take Rose to the doctor's office. As he continued on with his daily deliveries, his mind began to wander to Rose's situation and from there he began to think about Lara, and his previous marriage. Thinking about Rose both warmed and chilled his heart. Over the past two months, he'd grown quite fond of the young woman. He admired her tenacity and optimism. As time passed, he was becoming more invested in not just helping her, but her in general. Just her. It had been so long since he'd felt anything resembling fondness or… love for anyone. It was like an ice pick to his heart. Even considering caring about someone else felt like a betrayal to Lara. His wife.

Lara had been very different from Rose. Lara was outspoken, but absentminded. She'd often forget small objects like room keys lying about, whereas Rose was quiet and contemplative. But Gabriel had been taken with Lara immediately because though she was boisterous in a way most women weren't, she had a certain charm about her. Other men were always throwing themselves at her. Some desired her due to her outer beauty, and others were drawn in by her tendency to always say exactly what she was thinking, a tendency Gabriel had considered both a blessing and a curse.

Although many men had adored her, she was unaware of their constant presence. Men had flocked to her whenever she walked along the streets and went to the market—everywhere except where she worked. That's where Gabriel first noticed her. She was a handmaid at a hotel. Men didn't swarm around her there, trying to gain her attention because they believed that watching the lower-class work would somehow rub off on them and make them become lower-class. Every day, Gabriel visited her at the hotel. He'd been a member of the lower class for a long time before the stock market and his late father had handed him wealth. He kept his job for the wonderful people he got to see in the day. Not to mention, the only reason he was able to visit Lara in the city every day was that he was a courier, or as the upper class liked to call him "a lowly messenger boy". The hospital where he worked always had something to be delivered to the hotel, so he took advantage of his required deliveries to visit Lara. His job as courier afforded him many opportunities to visit her. When he wasn't delivering for the post office, he was dispersing medicine for the hospital. One day, when he was delivery medicine to the hotel owner as usual, Lara approached him and with eyes wide asked.

"I've seen you here almost every day, but I don't know your name. What is it?"

"It's Gabriel," he said, scrunching the package of medicine slightly in his nervousness. His heart was aflutter.

He finally decided to start courting Lara when another man tried to court her. She blatantly refused the burly man, but he didn't understand why. He was a man of high standing, and he was one of the few that didn't seem deterred by Lara's lower class job or the fact that she worked outside of the home. It would be an excellent chance to elevate her status, but perhaps that wasn't what she was interested in.

After he had finished his errands, he started heading back to his home with his horse pulling his carriage along, and was deep in thought about Lara's actions early that day, when he nearly ran into her. He'd ended up stopping for her and offering her a ride home. That night he asked her why she had turned down the other man's offer that day. Her response was, "It was the right words, but the wrong actions."

For a few months after that day he'd courted her. He'd bought her various gifts such as flowers and a necklace, and the mirror that he'd now given to Rose. He'd asked for her hand in marriage, and she'd accepted. Her parents hadn't approved at first, but Gabriel was determined. He wanted, no, he needed to be by her side.

After several months of convincing and dinners where he attempted to win over their good graces, he finally started to make some headway. Assisting them in household tasks went a long way in earning their trust. After several discussions about how a dowry wouldn't be needed because she's already won him over, they finally agreed. He was overjoyed at finally receiving a yes, and they agreed that they would marry immediately. She'd moved into his one bedroom house, and with their combined wages and his savings they were able to get a sizable house of their own.

However, only a short while after building a happy life in the new house, Lara fell ill. He brought her to the doctor in the city to try to find out what was wrong, but the doctor didn't know what ailed her. He took her to several other medical professionals, but none of them knew how to cure her. Some doctors theorized advanced rabies and said it was terminal. Others said that she seemed fine aside from a fever and suggested fluids and rest.

However, no matter the doctor, they couldn't agree upon a diagnosis. Sometimes, she would just rave at the mirror he'd given her, blaming it for her illness. He had tried hiding the mirror away, and even had someone else take it off his hands, but that didn't help. Lara was feverish and kept speaking of an evil man and a horrible deal in between incoherent maniacal babbling. As the illness progressed, she would get fevers so high that her body would writhe and seize up in the middle of the night. His heart became leaden with worry, and a recurrent fear crept into his thoughts. *I don't think she's going to get better.*

When it became too dangerous to keep taking her to different doctors, he took her back to their house. He quit his job and spent all of his time taking care of her. Much of his fortune went to trying to find a cure for Lara, but after only a few short weeks she became too weak to talk or leave her bed. Then one night, she went to bed and never opened her eyes again.

Gabriel was heartbroken by the loss, but refused to let it show. He became quieter and more withdrawn without Lara around.

That was two years before he met Rose. He was just starting to come out of his shell again. To live again. Now, it seemed history was repeating itself. Gabriel shook his head as he came out of his reverie.

"Stop thinking about Lara. She's not Lara," Gabriel said to himself.

When Gabriel looked around, he realized that in the time he'd been spaced out he'd finished his errands and was back at the house. He coaxed his horse to a stop and tied it up around the back of the house before heading inside, and was shocked by what he saw.

The entire house was spotless, and Rose was nowhere to be found.

CHAPTER 12

After Rose finished cleaning, her limbs began to ache. On a hunch, she dashed up the stairs to check on one of the roses she'd brought from the greenhouse. The bloom was almost completely wilted—its heavy head drooped over like a weary, old woman.

With deep sadness, Rose fingered the delicate blossom, causing one of the petals to flutter down to the windowsill. *I have to get back soon*, Rose thought to herself.

She frantically checked the rest of the house for more roses and found a few, but most of them were already wilted.

A lilting female voice echoed the words, *Come back to me, my Rose.* This irritated her mind like a mosquito that you can never swat away.

Rose tried to shake the voice off, but it continued to taunt her. *You can't escape your curse. You are bound to me,* it would say in teasing triumph. The connection to the voice suddenly snapped when the footfalls of Gabriel's horse sounded in the distance. She looped around to the front of the house just as Gabriel opened the door. She wanted to move from her hiding place, but something kept her ground to the spot.

He entered the house, and after a few moments whirled around and began searching outside.

"Rose are you near?" Gabriel called out.

His face awash with confusion, he walked around the outside of the house and started heading in her direction, but he didn't yet notice her. She started inching away quietly, but wasn't sure what was causing her to do so. In her attempt to sneak off, she barreled right into Gabriel's horse. Rose fell to the ground with a plop. This immediately alerted Gabriel to her presence when the horse started to whinny and buck from the commotion.

Rose panicked and ran away from the frantic horse…and straight into Gabriel.

"Rose are you well?" Gabriel asked. His face was tilted to one side. Eyes boring into her with unanswered questions.

"I am," Rose lied.

Her hands stiffened and a dull tightness prodded her chest. She covered her mouth and was greeted with the familiar tinge of blood on her hand.

Gabriel saw the blood, and he became stock still. His face became stern and solemn.

"You are not well Rose. I am taking you to the doctor," Gabriel said.

"What about the greenhouse?"

"If the doctor cures you, you shall no longer need the greenhouse."

"Then, I shall visit the doctor," Rose said.

Gabriel led her to the carriage, and they ventured into the city. When they reached the doctor's office several minutes later, he pulled her through the waiting room and into the doctor's room.

"Doctor, I brought the patient I told you about."

"Is she girl who resides in a greenhouse?" The doctor asked.

"Yes, this is Rose," Gabriel said.

"I take it that means the botanist wasn't helpful," He said with a raised eyebrow. When he was met with silence he said, "Okay, then we shall begin testing for her disease."

"Testing?" Rose asked. She gripped Gabriel's arm. Her eyes were wild with worry.

"It is so that he shall know how to cure you Rose," Gabriel said. He placed his hand over hers, giving it a slight squeeze of reassurance.

The doctor put his stethoscope to Rose's chest and said, "Take a deep breath in then breathe out."

Rose did what the doctor asked. He had her do some breathing exercises first. "Very good, Rose. Now, take a big breath in and hold it as long as you can." The doctor checked his pocket watch to measure how long she could hold her breath. Once she expelled the air and drew in a sharp inhale to refill her lungs, the doctor nodded and jotted something down on her chart. She complied as he checked her reflexes by tapping her lightly on the knees. Even when her throat, nose, and ears were probed she didn't flinch. "You have some slight irritation in the throat," he said.

The doctor had her repeat the exercise a few more times. Then he picked up a glass tube and a syringe. "Now, I need to get a sample of your blood."

Rose winced when the sharp point pricked her skin… As the doctor was examining her, she saw a puzzled look flit across his face, but it quickly disappeared when he saw her observing him. He grabbed her wrist and checked for a pulse and had her grip a small ball as hard as she could. When she struggled, the stiffness in her palms was evident. This time it was an obvious confused look. The doctor turned to Gabriel and said,

"May I speak with you outside please?"

Gabriel followed the doctor out of the room.

Rose quietly crept to the door and placed her ear against the small opening to listen in on their conversation, but they were speaking too low for her to hear.

☆ ☆ ☆

"I've never encountered any disease like Rose's. Her lungs and heart appear to be struggling for air, and her limbs are stiff. I'm going to make a list of all my observations then send you to some colleagues of mine. Perhaps, one of them may have encountered something like this before. For now, take Rose back to the greenhouse. It's probably the best place for her until we have more information on her condition," the doctor whispered.

"I shall take her back to the greenhouse immediately," Gabriel said.

The doctor finished jotting down his notes on a blank page just beneath Rose's chart, then he handed Gabriel the list of symptoms and directions to some other medical offices.

"Before we return, I must tell you that she's terrified of returning to the greenhouse. In order for her to go, it would be best if she believes

I will only be gone for a short while. Otherwise, she may refuse to return," Gabriel said.

With an understanding nod the doctor said, "If it's for the safety of the patient, then I understand. We will tell her that she is returning only until her prescription is received."

They both walked back in the room to tell Rose their version of the truth.

☆ ☆ ☆

"Rose, it seems you have a severe case of bronchitis. Gabriel is going to have to take you back to the greenhouse until we can get some medication for your condition. Gabriel is going to get your medicine from another office," The physician said somberly. Rose saw his clenched jaw and wondered if this news was difficult for him to deliver.

"Then, I suppose I shall live at the greenhouse once again," Rose said sadly. Her eyes searched Gabriel's and the physician's searching for a way out. She gripped the hospital bed, trying to hide the panic that ripped through her. The thought of being trapped in the greenhouse again made her want to run though she knew she wouldn't get very far.

Depression and disappointment laced her voice. She didn't want to go back to her glass prison, but perhaps it would be tolerable as long as it wasn't for an extended period.

"Shall we leave, Rose?" Gabriel asked.

"I suppose we shall," Rose said.

Uncertainty crept into her voice. She already regretted her decision of being marched back to her prison. Looking at Gabriel's concerned expression did nothing to ease her worries. Panic began to bubble up within her as she entered Gabriel's carriage. *Something's wrong,* was all Rose could think on the ride to the greenhouse. As they grew closer, Rose felt a scream building in her throat, but she refused to allow the feelings to overwhelm her. She wanted to trust Gabriel, but he refused to meet her gaze. His smile was gone, only a mockery of it remained. Her instincts told her to jump out of the carriage and run away from Gabriel. Her instincts told her that Gabriel was lying, but she didn't listen.

Polite as ever, Gabriel gently guided Rose into the greenhouse, holding the door open for her so she could enter. The uncertainty curled its claws further around her heart. The silence paralyzed her with fear.

"Gabriel may you promise me your return to this greenhouse?" Rose asked breaking the silence.

"I shall return so I may see my Rose again," Gabriel said.

For the first time since they'd met, he pressed his lips lightly to hers then gave her his trademark mischievous smile.

"That's a promise."

A blush rose to her cheeks at the unexpected kiss. It was enough to dispel some of her worries, to ignore that nagging voice in her mind. At that moment, Rose realized her Gabriel would always have her undivided attention, and endless adoration.

Chapter 13

Gabriel bolted to his buggy and sped off. The sooner he could find out what illness possessed Rose, the sooner he could return to her. He grabbed the parchment the doctor had given him and looked at the symptoms. The list read:

Patient's Symptoms:

Slight tightness in the chest

Coughing up blood

Stiffness of the limbs

Low pulse

Note: The patient's symptoms are vaguely reminiscent of chronic bronchitis, but I cannot be sure. I fear the last two symptoms cannot be explained by bronchitis. Her companion claims that her symptoms worsen when separated from the greenhouse near her parents' home. Please give any information on possible ailments to my messenger Gabriel.

Your Colleague,
Dr. Charles Robin

Gabriel took a look at the back of the letter and found the directions to the next doctor's office, and then he headed off to begin his search for a cure.

When Gabriel reached the town of Darkford, he began to take note of the differences from his own city. This city had squat houses all around, and a few miles off in the distance were factories that puffed filthy plumes of a dusty black smoke into the air. Poor men, women, and children were all around as he rode through the dirt paved streets. Some of them gawked at him, and others backed away in fear.

He nearly passed by the hospital. The only sign that the building held any practitioner of medicine was a small medical symbol recognizable from the twin snakes coiled around what appeared to be a needle with wings on the side of the front door.

When Gabriel entered the building, the smell of blood and death assaulted his senses. A man with a stethoscope in his hand and blood on his clothing approached him. The sight, combined with scent, reminded Gabriel of the former poor conditions of the hospital where he worked. He started to back away reflexively, for the sake of his own health. Years ago, doctors didn't realize their carelessness about cleanliness was responsible for many deaths by infection. This place screamed of dirtiness and risk. Before he'd retreated too far, Gabriel remembered why he was there. He halted and stood his ground.

"Hello, dear boy, what is it you need?" the doctor asked with a smile.

"I have a message for you, doctor," Gabriel said.

"Ah you must be a courier. What message do you bear?" the doctor asked.

"A patient in the town over is experiencing strange symptoms. Your colleague is unaware of what her illness may be. Do you know of an illness with these symptoms?"

Gabriel handed the doctor the paper with the symptoms on it and after a few moments of scanning over the paper the doctor handed it back to him and said, "I believe the symptoms are quite similar to a combination of arthritis and chronic bronchitis, but you should get the opinion of another doctor to be certain."

Gabriel sighed and began to walk out of the doctor's office. He grabbed his list from Dr. Robin and put a line through the first address on the list, a dead end.

As he made his way towards the exit, he ran into a little boy. The child was robed in rags and his hair was a matted mess. With a toothy smile that had plentiful gaps, he held out his hands to Gabriel in anticipation. Gabriel couldn't help but pity the boy. He dropped a silver coin into the boys waiting hands. The boy's eyes widened. For a moment, he just stood there paralyzed by disbelief. Then, his smile grew even wider, and he ran off with the money, towards a woman dressed in clothing as worn down as the beggar boys.

He handed her the money, and she smiled as well. For a while, their mouths moved as they conversed. The boy pointed to Gabriel. They both turned to Gabriel and waved. Gabriel smiled and waved back then walked to his carriage and set off to the next town.

It took Gabriel several weeks in his carriage to make it to the next doctor. He'd been forced to stop at a nearby town during the trek because, as he had neared the town, his horse's pace had become slower, and he figured it needed time to rest. Then, he continued on to the next town. As he grew closer to the next destination, he began to notice a thick smog closing in on him.

There were many houses here, as there were in the other doctor's town, but in this place the dwellings looked slightly less impoverished. The buildings seemed just a backdrop for the excessively large factories. Both factories had chimneys that towered over all the buildings in town and rose to quadruple the height of any house or other building. The smokestacks billowed toxic plumes as black as night into the air.

Few people ventured into the deathly fumes that surrounded the factory. Those that did were factory workers, recognizable by their dirt and soot coated bodies. Many people wore masks that covered their noses and mouths or covered their mouths with small cloths. In this town, there was a constant chorus of violent coughs.

Gabriel was intrigued and disgusted by the mess of a city. He was so zoned in to the change in atmosphere that he almost ran over one of the townspeople. Gabriel tried to make the horse come to a sudden stop, but the horse was through taking orders. The horse bucked violently in response, causing him and the cart to topple over. A crunching sound reverberated through his leg, and a sharp pain echoed through him. He tried to get up, but was only rewarded with a cracking sound, followed by another wave of agony. He screamed out in pain as he cradled his leg. The horse righted itself, then stormed off, running away with his money, his health, and his method of transportation.

☆ ☆ ☆

Off in the distance, the citizen that Gabriel had almost run over morphed shape and moved out of sight. His skin was translucent. His aura was as toxic as the factory's fumes. If Gabriel didn't want to use the potion, then Nightshade would delay him… or kill him.

☆ ☆ ☆

Somehow Gabriel had managed to keep the list in his hand, but knew it wouldn't do him much good if the wound was fatal, so he limped his way to a building with a line full of people. He tapped one of the people in line on the shoulder and asked,

"Where is the hospital?" and the effort made him gasp in pain.

The person turned around to respond, a middle-aged man with a small silvering beard.

"This is the line for the hospital," He said and eyed Gabriel with suspicion.

"Why do you need to know?"

"I'm a courier from a few towns over. I've come to deliver a message to the doctor," Gabriel said, purposely ignoring the topic of his own injuries.

"Good luck getting through this line. I've been waiting here for many hours," the middle-aged man replied.

"Well, I guess I shall have to enter as if I have the right to bypass this line."

Gabriel began to elbow his way through the crowd. Those with contagious diseases were absent, and he guessed that they had already been ushered in. Many had lacerations on their arms. Some were missing limbs, likely from factory accidents. Some were coughing uncontrollably. Their faces lacked color. He received a few disgruntled comments and aggravated noises, but no one stopped him from pushing through the crowd. Many gaped at the severity of his injuries.

When Gabriel finally managed to enter the doors of the hospital, he was concerned. This place only looked slightly cleaner than the last hospital. There were no bloody or reused bandages being used, and the doctors were sanitizing the wounded to prevent infection. However, several doctors still wore clothing coated in blood and other bodily fluids. The hospital still stank of sickness and grime. He limped his way to one of the workers there and asked where the doctor was.

"He's over in the room just down the hall, but—" The man began to say.

But the worker's voice trailed off as Gabriel rushed away from the man and towards the door he'd pointed at. When Gabriel finally reached the door, he shoved it open without warning or pretense, and the door creaked open. His good knee gave way from carrying his full weight on its own, and he fell to his palms just a couple of feet away from an aggravated, onlooking doctor with surprisingly clean attire.

The doctor's expression turned from the glare of anger to the furrowed brow of concern when he noticed the unnatural twist to Gabriel's right leg. He abruptly dashed out of the room, and when he returned there were a few more people at his side. One carried a jar of clear liquid, and another carried bandages. Surprisingly, none of them carried an amputation saw. An assistant handed the doctor something they called ether. He took a long inhale and the pain coursing through him dulled. Gabriel felt the faint prickle of alcohol being poured on his leg and the dulled pain of the bone in his leg being set. Then, he watched as the doctor wrapped up his leg tightly in a thick, damp cloth.

When Gabriel had finally regained full reign of his senses, the assistants were gone, but the doctor was still there scanning over him. In his hand was a bloodied piece of paper, the doctor's note.

He scanned it, and as if it were just an afterthought said to Gabriel, "Oh Gabriel you've finally regained some sense. Your leg was broken. We set the bone, but you should keep off your feet as much as possible for the next few months, and as for this letter…most doctors around here would say diphtheria, but that seems unlikely to me because if you've been around her, you probably would've caught the disease. I believe that a more likely diagnosis is a combination of poliomyelitis and bronchitis. Poliomyelitis would explain the sudden paralysis, and bronchitis would explain having trouble breathing and coughing up blood. The only symptom here that puzzles me is the lower pulse. I'll write my diagnosis on here, and you can take it back to the doctor in your town, once your leg is healed."

"But I have to get back to Rose… I mean, to the doctor. What if her condition gets worse?"

"Then, I'll have someone send the diagnosis over to the doctor."

"But, the doctor doesn't know where she lives, and she will not let the doctor into her house."

The doctor gave Gabriel a disbelieving look, then caught a side-long glance at Gabriel and shook his head in a brief moment of understanding. He leaned closer to Gabriel and said,

"I understand you want to get back to your mistress, but it's not safe for you to travel long distances until you're completely healed. The next doctor that could fix a broken leg, without amputating it or killing you, is several months travel by foot. Trust me, lad, if she cares she'll still be there. Until then, focus on healing."

Gabriel tried to get up and cringed in pain so the doctor handed him a cane.

"Also, I'd suggest you find some work that doesn't require much walking. You're going to be in this town for a while. Perhaps, you can be this town's courier?"

"That's a greatly appreciated offer, sir." Gabriel took the cane and turned to leave.

"Here's the doctor's letter," the doctor said and handed it to Gabriel before he walked out of the office, leaning heavily on his cane.

CHAPTER 14

When Rose had been returned by Gabriel, her mother had immediately sniffed her out like a bloodhound. Lailah rushed in, her face practically glowing as she said "I'm so glad you're safe. It appears that someone had the good sense to bring you back home where you belong," she said.

"This isn't my home! It hasn't been since you let that monster near me, and yet you still allow him in your dungeon of a house. You put us both at risk!" Rose snapped.

Something in Lailah cracked. Her face was now emotionless, impassive. She silently strode out of the room without another word.

That had been a month ago. She'd kept time by observing the moon. One full moon cycle had passed since Gabriel left. Her mother seemed by instinct to know that Rose no longer had anyone to escape to. When Lailah had visited the greenhouse yesterday to give Rose her monthly food supply, her head was held high and the victory in her gaze could've smote the finest bull. At that point, Rose must have been ignorant to some nuance that gave her mother this confidence. Rose hadn't become concerned until she'd realized the second month was drawing near and he still hadn't returned. Every time her mother would bring her something, and find her still lingering in the greenhouse, she would straighten her back a little more and Rose would slump lower to the ground.

Rose began speaking to her reflection in the beautiful mirror that Gabriel had given her. Seeing it, though, was a painful reminder of him. It was a remnant of the brief taste of freedom that had slipped through her fingers.

Gazing at the mirror she'd reassure herself, "He'll be back soon, right? I wonder how he's doing now. What had the new doctor said to him?" she'd ask. A questioning look would reflect back.

CHAPTER 15

After being bandaged up by the doctor, Gabriel went limping with his new cane. He had pondered trying to return to Rose. He had the funds, but the doctor was right. He definitely couldn't risk it on foot and, even with the horse, a long journey could aggravate his wounds. He didn't want to risk becoming an amputee if he got an infection. The medical staff in the nearby towns would likely amputate his wounds, not to mention throwing money around could raise unwanted attention for him. He resigned himself to staying here, at least until he had healed.

The doctor offered him money to assist with some simple deliveries, but he also knew he would need a horse to get around. He surely couldn't do the deliveries on foot.

He went over to the nearest post office and asked for work. After some puzzled looks from the staff, he explained his situation and previous experience in his hometown. In response the staff said "Okay. We'll let you borrow a horse and you can run some deliveries for us on a temporary basis."

Gabriel nodded, "I'll take the job. Thank you for your kindness."

He accepted the two smaller jobs and the borrowed horse and then went in search of an apartment. Finding an apartment proved difficult, so in the meantime he stayed at the local inn. His lucky break came when the doctor got a lead on an open apartment from a friend. He began working, allowing himself to heal so he could find his way back to Rose soon.

CHAPTER 16

Time started to blend together. She'd stopped tracking time and feared the passage of another day or week. Her conversations became bitter. Sometimes, her reflection now answered back.

"It's your own fault that you're trapped here. You shouldn't have trusted him," she said to her reflection.

It answered back with, "Well, you wanted to fawn over the local courier. With a mischievous smile like his, how did you not know he was trouble?" She would hold the mirror and stare back at her own reflection with disgust or detachment.

In Rose's now warped thoughts, it felt like it had been many years though that seemed unlikely. She felt the same hopelessness creeping in as from before she met Gabriel.

"Why must you be so unworthy of affection? Why would you think a man like Gabriel would want you when your own mother can't stand you? What is it that makes you hideous? Is it a personality trait or your useless burnt hands?" Rose ranted to her reflection and in her mind she heard.

"Or perhaps there's nothing wrong with you my dear. Perhaps you were simply never meant to leave this greenhouse. You were meant to live amongst the plants, for even they require company."

Rose heard that voice like a wind whistling lightly in her ear. She recognized the sound. It was the same voice from her dream.

"Why would plants need my company? Surely, each other's company is enough."

"But they have no means of communication. All they wish is to be given a voice through human tongue."

"You say this as if you're a plant yourself."

"I only understand the plants. I'm not their voice."

Rose knew this was all the answer she'd get. She put down the mirror, and returned to her makeshift house, her hands shaking like leaves in the wind.

52

CHAPTER 17

After two months of work, Gabriel's leg began to heal. He had saved some money from his new jobs as well. That's when he knew it was time to head back to Rose.

He wondered if she would still be in her greenhouse waiting for him or if she'd run off and… he knew well what would have happened if she had escaped on her own, but he quickly brushed the thought from his mind as he strolled over to the marketplace.

As he drew closer, a hoard of tents and booths came into view, and he began to hear the call of salespeople.

"Canned goods!"

"Cheap produce!"

"Old jewelry!"

These were some songs of the salesmen, but he ignored their calls. Eventually he got close enough to hear the sales pitch he wanted to hear.

"The finest horses in town!"

It was music to his ears. Gabriel headed towards the seller's booth and started up a conversation with the wiry young man that manned the booth.

"Do you have any horses worth two months' salary?"

"That all depends. What is your occupation?"

"A courier," Gabriel replied, purposely keeping off the fact that he'd been making extra money by assisting the doctor. He knew salesman were leeches and would try to suck every penny he owned from him, but he couldn't afford to spend all of his money. He still needed to buy a new carriage on his way back.

The man let out a low laugh and called the other salesman out from the stables.

"This messenger boy here wants to try to buy a horse," the wiry man said.

"Does he have any money," the other man asked.

The salesmen were aggravating Gabriel. He needed that horse quickly and didn't have time to play games, so he took out two months of his real salary, much more than he'd intended, and said to the salesman,

"Yes I do as a matter of fact." then dropped the money into the other salesman's hand.

The other salesman looked at the money and his expression turned from amusement to shock. He looked from the money to Gabriel and back again, and then ran back into the stables. When the salesman finally returned, he had with him the finest looking horse Gabriel had ever seen. It had a silky black mane of hair with powerful rippling muscles in its legs. However, the looks didn't mean the salesmen weren't tricking him into buying a lame horse. Now, it was his turn to play games. He'd bought enough horses to know what he was doing.

"He is a mighty fine looking horse. But, before I buy him may I take a closer look at him?"

"Certainly sir," The salesman said trembling slightly at Gabriel's piercing gaze and venomous smile.

Gabriel went over to the horse and started by systematically picking up his feet and tapping on each of his horseshoes to see if the horse would spook or show signs of pain, then he pulled at the bit lightly to test his gums. Nothing happened during either test, so now it was time to see his stride.

"May I take the horse for a light tread?"

"C-c-certainly sir," The salesman stuttered.

Gabriel mounted the horse and gradually moved him into a canter. *Still no sign of weakness, but his gait is a little slow,* Gabriel thought.

He slowed the horse down to a trot again and brought the horse back to the salesmen. Without dismounting he said, "This horse will do quite nicely gentlemen. I'll take it."

Gabriel rode out of the market atop his new horse, back to his hometown.

CHAPTER 18

After months back in her glass cage, Rose had grown weary of everything. Her once bright hopes of freedom had withered, much like her roses had when she plucked them from the greenhouse. She was in need of amusement. Rose was sick of the arrogant smile her mother wore each time she visited, so Rose decided to give mother dearest a little scare.

As Lailah's footsteps approached, Rose hid behind her makeshift house to see her mother's reaction. Her mother carried a carton of milk and a basket of eggs. Lailah got closer and closer, picking up the pace when she didn't see Rose there.

The greenhouse door opened and she heard her mother's call.

"Rose? Rose are you here? Where are you?"

When there was no reply, her brow creased in worry. Lailah put down the food and started scrambling around the greenhouse looking for any sign that Rose had left. When her mother's back was turned, Rose grabbed the food and took her spot back behind the makeshift house.

When Lailah turned around, she noticed the food was gone and worry turned to aggravation. "Very funny Rose you can come out now."

Her mother placed her hands on her hips and rolled her eyes, and then Rose emerged from behind her small abode. Her mother's smug smile was gone, but she could still sense that feeling of superiority coming off her mother in waves.

"Why are you so happy that I haven't left?" Rose asked.

"Because I care about your safety, Rose."

Rose heard the lie in her voice. She wanted to know the truth, but she wasn't willing to push her mother any further.

CHAPTER 19

Gabriel had bought a new carriage from the doctor. Apparently, the hospital had kept one from their old courier. Even after the courier had left the town, they'd kept the carriage. As Gabriel was leaving the hospital, Gabriel was stopped by the doctor that had healed him.

The doctor gave Gabriel a small pill box and said, "This is for Rose."

"What is it for?"

"To help with painful breathing. She must mix the powder with water and take it once a day. We may need to add additional medicine to account for the stiffness if that symptom worsens."

Gabriel turned the small cylindrical container in his hand. He could see that whatever the doctor had given him was a yellow powdery substance. *It won't work. You should just give her the medicine you already have. No one knows curses better than me,* the familiar dark voice echoed in his mind. He pushed it aside.

"Thank you, doctor," Gabriel said with hesitation creeping into his voice.

"Where is this carriage?" Gabriel asked eager to change the subject.

"It's around the back of the hospital. Please allow me to lead you to it."

Gabriel complied, allowing the doctor to lead him to the carriage. It was a light wood, probably oak, and it had a thick coat of dust on its surface. In its center was an almost too conveniently placed saddle. It looked as if it had seen no use in months, maybe years.

"Are you sure it's functional?"

"Not entirely, but you may put it to use for no charge," the doctor said with a smile.

Something about this smile made Gabriel choke back suspicion at this offer. Maybe it was just the dark voices influence, but he knew well that nothing in life was ever cheap and certainly never free unless there were strings attached. At the current moment, he couldn't afford his suspicions.

"Then I will give it good use," Gabriel said and began dragging the glorified wheelbarrow back to his waiting horse.

The doctor followed behind him and watched all the while as Gabriel saddled up his horse, then tethered it to the carriage. Then, the doctor watched Gabriel force the old carriage into motion. Behind the doctor, Gabriel swore that he saw the outline of the man that had been tormenting his thoughts, but maybe it was just his imagination.

CHAPTER 20

Rose gazed into the mirror Gabriel had given her, as had become her obsession. In the reflective pane, she saw something. It was her, but not her. She was in the greenhouse. Her dress was no longer white. In the glass, her clothing was dirty. That Rose paced back and forth across the greenhouse, yelling at the plants, as if they could actually answer her. Her reflection looked rabid, feverish. Her hair was wild. Several strands stuck straight up or flew free, and it was horribly tangled. Her eyes were constantly darting around searching for an enemy that wasn't there.

It was pacing back and forth in the greenhouse, yelling at the plants *"You've ruined my life, but you're the only thing keeping me alive, and I hate you for it!"* Rose tuned into the mirror as her crazed self cursed when her hands fumbled with the hose handle.

This version of her threw the watering can down in frustration to let it land by the hose. It yelled at the white roses in her garden, *"Why have you doomed me to this fate? You have made me crippled and bound me to this horrible place. I can't even hurt you because you don't have feelings. You can't even argue when I yell at you. You're useless! I can't even kill you because I would just be killing myself."*

Her crazed self sat on the ground seething with anger, flicking at the roses' white petals. Then, she stood up and mumbled, *"I'll be back to deal with you later,"* before stomping into her makeshift house…

The image of herself swirled in the mirror and was replaced by a pair of forest green eyes. They were darker and wilder than the spheres that were Gabriel's emerald green eyes.

"Was that me?" Rose said to herself.

"It is the fever that will consume you if you let it," The woman's voice said, and the truth in her words sent a shiver down Rose's spine. The eyes disappeared leaving Rose staring back at her own reflection. Her ember colored eyes were filled with confusion and fear.

CHAPTER 21

Gabriel made it to the nearest town a couple of days later. He managed to tie up his horse and make it back to his wooden cart of a carriage before he collapsed to the floor of the cart in utter exhaustion. He fell into a dreamless sleep, but slowly something dark crept into his sleeping mind. In a swirl of fog, he appeared in his childhood room, but the room felt eerie, wrong. The form of what Gabriel only dimly recognized as his mother appeared before him. Her eyes burned with fever, and her hair was wild and matted in sweat. Her emerald green eyes mirrored his, and they were burning into him.

"Why did you kill me, my child?" she shrieked, her voice a pain filled moan. Her skeletal arm reached out for him. The flesh peeled off of her fingers and worked its way up her arm. It flitted away and dissolved into the air. The decay continued its way up her arm seizing her chest.

The woman broke into crazed laughter. Her face melted and reformed into his late wife's face. Her eyes begged for mercy. They seemed to know what lie ahead. She approached Gabriel but when she spoke it was a man's voice.

"This will happen to her, too…unless you leave her."

Gabriel reached out to touch her and the image of Lara began to writhe and squirm. When it turned to him, it was a twisted mockery of Rose's face.

"Leave me before it's too late!" the figure shrieked, and when he didn't respond it gave him a malicious smile.

Gabriel felt his face twitch. The dim room became unfocused as the light faded to darkness.

He bolted upright in his carriage, heart racing. The cart jerked to the side from the sudden movement. It was to a darkening sky that he awoke with that smile still burned into his mind.

CHAPTER 22

Rose tried once again to water the greenhouse plants because if she didn't, then the plants would die. That wouldn't bode well for her. She tried to will her useless hands to cooperate and close around the knob. Ever since her failed escape attempt, her hands were not fully functional. With a sigh of frustration, she fumbled with the garden hose a few times before she actually managed to get it turned on. In triumph, she proceeded to fill the watering can.

As water reached the top, she scrambled for the knob again. She had to get the hose shut off before she covered herself in water and mud. Again. One fumble... two fumbles...got it. She paused for a moment as she realized that she felt almost content with her life in the greenhouse without her mother around. Her mother had begun visiting less when Rose had taken to talking to the mirror. She had distanced herself, as if afraid Rose was contagious. Her mother was overbearing and the dark shadow looming over her, frightening. Rose felt free, like a chain was removed from her ankle. When she was alone, Rose admitted it was almost as if she was born to be amongst flowers.

Rose let the thought settle in her brain as she cared for the plants of the greenhouse. *If he doesn't come back maybe I could learn to like it here,* she thought as she settled to the ground next to her white roses.

CHAPTER 23

Gabriel ran his hand through his short, thick, golden hair, a nervous habit of his.

What was that dream about? Gabriel thought as he paced near the carriage.

He barely remembered his mother, but from his foggy recollection of her. She'd looked so much like that fevered image. She shared his golden skin, and her emerald green eyes were a perfect replica of his own. He wasn't surprised by the chocolate brown hair. He knew that his lighter hair color came from his father, but he was shocked that they'd looked so alike. They even shared the same sharp facial features that, on him, made him look edgy and on her, he imagined would have taken on a more elegant air if he had seen her when she wasn't consumed by fever. She'd died of illness only a few years after his birth.

His father had told him that in the end she'd been deliriously ranting about a curse and tried to kill Gabriel in his crib while he was sleeping. The doctor's tried everything, but in the end the sickness took his mother. Gabriel's father raised him until he was old enough to work, and then he'd left for the army. He hadn't seen his father since.

As Gabriel untied the horse, so he could continue his travels, his thoughts began to drift off to Rose. He wondered if she would understand the reason for his prolonged departure or if she would be worked into a fury.

CHAPTER 24

Maybe, it was all in her mind, but Rose had become easily frustrated in the last few days. This morning she had lived out a scene almost identical to the mirror. She'd fumbled with the hose, and after what felt like the twelfth fumble, she'd thrown the hose and watering can down in a blind rage. Then, she'd begun yelling at the roses with such fervor that she was glad the poor flowers weren't able to talk back. In childish protest, Rose announced that she'd "be back to deal with them later" and stomped off, slamming the door to her tiny bedroom and fuming like a stubborn child.

Now, she was sitting on a small wooden chair in her bedroom, shivering as she wondered what would happen if her mind warped completely. She wished that somehow Gabriel could fix the situation, but her hopes that he would return anytime soon had grown dim.

The strange woman had entered Rose's thoughts and dreams, and she was finally starting to win this mental fight even though the back of her mind cried out not to let *her* win.

CHAPTER 25

It had been two weeks since the first nightmare, and with every small town that brought him closer to Rose, the nightmares only got worse. The most recent one had included a woman with forest green eyes…

The woman was clothed in leaves and jagged wings, like the opening of a Venus flytrap graced her back. Her eyes burned with hatred as they bore into Gabriel. She glared at Gabriel and snarled *"Don't come any closer to Rose. You're an abomination, a raging fire out to destroy the only Rose left in my forest!"* Then, a man with endless, black pits for eyes appeared. The smog of hate in the woman's eyes became a maelstrom. The man tried to charm the woman, saying, *"We could be the ultimate pair, once again. We'll rule over nature and human industry alike."* His efforts just made his putrid nature shine through. She backed away from him, nose scrunched up in distaste. At the rejection, he said, *"That's fine. I'll win again like I always do, and I'll take your precious Rose away from you, too."* Her eyes latched onto his throat like a wolf going in for the kill, and she jumped on the man lashing out at him in a blind fury. The man was caught unexpectedly, and she hit him head on and sent him toppling to the misty ground of the dream. Her nails clawed at his throat and her legs pinned him to the ground. One of her hands pinned both of his hands above his head. Just when Gabriel thought the woman was grabbing the upper hand, the strange man managed to get an arm free and punched the woman in the gut. She loosened her grip and he bucked her off of him. The woman fell to the floor, cringing, and there was a dark cloud lingering where he had touched her.

"Now that you've been injured, your precious Rose will be susceptible to my curse until you find some way to heal."

After that they both disappeared, but the man's last statement was so smug, like he was sure she wouldn't be able to recover from the injury he'd dealt her. Gabriel was left wondering how and why the creatures of his dreams were fighting over Rose.

CHAPTER 26

Rose moved about the greenhouse, watering can in hand, as she sprinkled the plants. She'd just lifted the metal spout over the roses when she doubled over in pain. Dropping the can, she clutched her stomach. It was almost like an invisible force had punched her in the gut. For a few moments, she was stuck on the ground gasping in pain grabbing her stomach as she worked through the sudden pain. Eventually, the pain subsided, and she got back up. Leaving her wondering what had just happened. Her eyes darted around the greenhouse looking for her invisible tormentor.

When the pain full subsided, Rose lifted herself from the ground and with a shrug went back to watering the roses in her garden.

CHAPTER 27

As Gabriel drew closer to his home village, he slept less and less. He only succumbed to it when his body gave out from exhaustion. Even then, he only rested until a nightmare entered his mind. He'd wake up flailing and gasping for air, pinching himself to make sure he was still alive and awake. It had been a few weeks on the road, and dark circles began to form under his eyes. Riding for more than a few hours caused his head to bob up and down. Evading sleep was a constant struggle. The floral scent of the roses, her brilliant smile, these were the only thing spurring him onward.

He was one town away from the site of his old job, but his head continued to bob. At one point, he was awoken by the neighing of his horse and barely pulled the reins fast enough to stop himself from running right over a child. He knew he needed to rest. So, with head bowed in defeat, he tied his horse up, located the nearest inn, and purchased a room. He trudged up the stairs, opened the door, and barely managed to close it behind him before exhaustion took over and he collapsed onto the bed. A silent prayer slid from his lips that the man with the soulless eyes wouldn't enter his dreams this night.

"You can't escape the curse."

Without turning around Gabriel knew he was about to see the dark eyes of the strange man again.

"Lovely, yet another night I will have to forgo sleep because a lunatic with cabin fever has decided I need to be woken with his mumbles of curses and other such crackpot chatter," Gabriel mumbled to himself then turned around to face the dark eyed man.

"What could you possibly want this time?"

"What? You aren't happy to see your nightly haunt?"

"No. I was actually planning on getting some sleep tonight, so why don't you beat it?" Gabriel said, and narrowed his eyes at the man.

"Although, I suppose you have other plans for me."

"No, I just figured I'd bother you now that you don't have that weak woman protecting your dreams. She's too busy nursing some nasty wounds." The strange man flashed Gabriel a wicked smile.

"Why bother me now when you've had so many years to be a complete and utter bastard?" spat Gabriel.

"Because, entering your dreams wasn't necessary, that is, until you found a woman that was being protected by a certain creature with forest green eyes. Watch your tongue or I might drag out the death of this Rose of yours. So long kid."

The strange man turned around with a wave of dismissal and disappeared before Gabriel could ask what he meant about killing Rose.

How could he kill Rose or anyone else real, Gabriel thought.

Gabriel awoke to the sun streaming through the windows of his room. He'd actually managed to sleep through the night, but he was left with more questions than he'd had from any of his other nightmares.

Rose couldn't seem to sleep. Something was making her anxious. She'd been pacing the greenhouse all night with the mirror Gabriel had given her as if she thought maybe it would show her the answer. But, all she saw was her own haggard face. Over the course of the last week, dark circles had become a prominent feature underneath her eyes. Her red tinged black hair had become matted and worn from her pulling at it and running her fingers through it as she suffered through several nervous breakdowns. She was falling apart at the seams.

Now, she didn't even wish for Gabriel to return. She just wanted the voice in her head to stop driving her over the cliff of insanity. The mirror tore at her sanity, showing her a future she wasn't prepared to accept, and the woman's voice taunted her. As she watched the sunrise, she prayed it all would end soon.

☆ ☆ ☆

As the sun began to dominate the sky, Gabriel headed back to the first doctor. He guessed that, by now, his former position was gone, but he'd find other work somehow. He walked to his horse's post from last night and was relieved to find it awaiting his return. As he untied the horse with care, he imagined how Rose must be feeling and frowned. He looked down at the ground, chastising himself. He should have returned sooner.

Gabriel mounted his horse and set off to the doctor's office, feeling for the note in his pocket, and hoping that the doctor could find some kind of cure for Rose.

Gabriel pulled up to the doctor's office in his rag-tag carriage and tied it near the front door. He passed a mirror on the way in and noticed how run down he looked. A thick layer of stubble covered his chin and cheeks. His face was paper-white and his clothing was dirty and tattered. With a shake of his head and a shrug of his shoulders, Gabriel moved past the mirror and pushed open the door to the doctor.

The doctor was standing there, and gawked at Gabriel for a few moments taking in his current state.

"I've brought you back the notes from the other doctors," Gabriel said, jaw clenched. He needed answers and this man was his last hope.

"What caused it to take so long? You were gone for several months," The doctor's curiosity edged his tone.

"It's a long story," Gabriel said, waving it off with a shrug.

He handed the Dr. Robin the note, and his shocked look turned to thoughtfulness as he examined the other doctors' recommendations.

"These are all possible, but none of them explain why the symptoms would only appear when she leaves that greenhouse. I'm afraid there's nothing I can do."

At that, Gabriel cursed under his breath, snatched the note from Dr. Robin, and stormed out of the office. He hastily untied his horse and headed off to the greenhouse. He hoped the medicine from the other doctor would help.

The sound of his horse's hooves against the unpaved roads just seemed to ramp his heart rate up a notch. The closer he got to the greenhouse, the more nervous he became. He kept running through all of Rose's possible reactions to his late arrival. Would she feel betrayal because he hadn't returned as soon as he'd promised, or anger because he couldn't find a cure? He ran through all the scenarios, but what he found was a possibility he'd never anticipated.

CHAPTER 28

Rose thought she had to be dreaming when she saw what appeared to be Gabriel approaching her greenhouse. After so much time had passed, the pitiful hope she'd clung to that he would return had shriveled and died, leaving confusion and betrayal instead. Now, she was skeptical about why he'd bothered to return at all.

Her mind's recollection of Gabriel was…wrong. The Gabriel of her memory hadn't worn ragged clothing. His horse had been different. The carriage she'd ridden in with him was much better than this wheelbarrow of a cart he had now. This definitely had to be a dream. She expected to wake up at any moment. But she didn't.

This bedraggled Gabriel approached her. He walked with a slight limp. Rose frowned, wondering what had happened to him. She watched intently as he opened the greenhouse door. She sized him up like a predator would its prey, waiting for him to talk, so she could pounce on his excuses, yell at this false Gabriel like she never would have with the real one.

"Rose? Are you well?" Gabriel asked.

He held a glass bottle filled with a yellow powdery looking substance in one hand and what looked like a note in the other hand. Rose didn't wait for him to spout the lame excuses she knew were coming.

"What do you mean, am I well? I've been locked up in this glass prison for an eternity with only a mirror and some plants for company. My own mother is avoiding me like the plague. She delivers my food when she thinks I'm sleeping. Tiptoeing in, then running back out. I'm losing my mind," she shrieked, eyes blazing.

CHAPTER 29

Gabriel was taken aback.

She's lost her mind, Gabriel thought. Normally, he'd back away from a situation like this, but he felt defensive about his extended leave. Anger bubbled up within him. Coming out in sarcasm that laced his every word.

"I was just wasting my time ignoring you. It's not like my leg was broken by my own carriage. It's not like my horse ran off with that carriage. It's not like my leg was almost amputated because of the damage. It's not like I've been trying to get you a cure for over a year and only have this." He paused and shook the bottle with the yellow substance in front of her face.

He leaned closer until each of his breaths touched her face. "But, go ahead and take out your anger on the person trying to help you," he said. His tone was flat, cold.

At this Rose was puzzled. She was still unsure if this was the real Gabriel or just her mind playing tricks, but some gut instinct made her want to test this theory.

"I'd consider apologizing if this were real, but at any moment, I'll awake to my endless imprisonment."

Rose never ceased to amaze him. He pulled back his face from hers and gave her a look that was exasperated and puzzled.

"You think this is all pretend?" Gabriel said.

"If it isn't, prove to me this is real."

He leaned in close to her face with his eyes shuttered as if he were about to kiss her. Rose paused her ranting and raving in anticipation and instead of feeling his lips on hers, she felt a sharp pain on her arm and looked down to see Gabriel pinching her.

"I guess you are real. Only the real you would do something so underhanded and childish," Rose said with a sigh and rolled her eyes at him.

"You left me no other choice. You were absolutely mad!" He argued, but a slight smile curved his lips, betraying his tone.

"Well pardon me. Being secluded in a greenhouse will do that to you. You should try it some time," Rose said, stomping off.

"I'm the childish one?" Gabriel called after her, then followed her into her makeshift house. "So, are you going to let me tell you about what happened now?"

"What and spoil the bickering?" Rose retorted.

Gabriel sighed and continued. "Well the truth is…there was no prescription. I went out looking for a cure, but I didn't have much luck. In one of the towns, I fell off my horse, and it ran off with my belongings and the carriage."

He skimmed over the time he'd spent in the last town, not wanting to worry her about how he'd managed to get home.

"I also got the medicine that I waved in front of your face from the last doctor on my trip, but our local doctor said the medicine wouldn't work because it doesn't match your symptoms. In the end, I couldn't bring back any medicine for you," he said sadly and tore his gaze from hers.

He didn't want to see her disappointment. In the end, he didn't tell her about the strange man haunting him in his sleep. Her talk of dreams and insanity made him believe his nightmares were becoming reality.

He touched the vial in his pocket. The one he'd gotten from the man in the greenhouse. *If you use it, I will require a favor. If you refuse, a great misfortune will fall upon you.* The words echoed in his mind. He might need the vial after all.

CHAPTER 30

Rose could see dark circles forming under Gabriel's eyes. He looked worse off than her. Even his typical smile looked tired, forced. She wanted to ask what was wrong, but when he didn't mention the reason for his current state, and when her fiery gaze met his frozen emerald stare, she knew he was intent on leaving that part of the story out. She wasn't willing to push him to tell her.

"We should leave," Rose said.

Gabriel avoided Rose's gaze. She took this as a sign that maybe he'd given up on escape. She gave him an out.

"But if you wish to leave me, I'd understand."

At this Gabriel lifted his gaze to hers. His face was contorted with pain. Maybe she'd misjudged him.

Gabriel once again touched the mysterious potion from the botanist. "...I did receive one possible cure, but it comes from a questionable source. It was from a botanist that lives as a hermit on the edge of town."

He pulled out the reddish liquid from his pocket and handed it to her. "But there's a—"

She placed her hand out, cutting him off. "I don't care about its origins as long as I can escape this wretched prison!"

She gulped down the vial in one fell swoop.

No sooner had she drank the potion than her face became flushed, and her skin dried and turned a reddish hue. She swayed on her feet and screamed out babbling about freedom and then suddenly fell to the ground in a heap. Her pupils turned to saucers, and she writhed on the floor briefly before falling completely silent.

"No! What have you done?"

Gabriel heard a scream and an ethereal shape materialized. She was clothed in plants and her hair was silver. Her eyes were wild in panic.

"That's no cure. That's the juice of the sorcerer's cherry. She'll be dead in a few days, maybe less."

Gabriel's eyes widened at the woman's sudden appearance. "Who are you, and why should I trust you?"

"My name is Belladonna. I'm a nymph, and I gave her mother, Lailah, a potion that helped her birth Rose."

"Is there any way I can help her?"

"There is one way, but it'll be dangerous for a human like you," she said as her eyes narrowed.

"I'll do whatever it takes. Just tell me what to do."

"There's a tree called the Manchineel tree that holds the key to saving her, but you must proceed with caution. Everything on the tree from the leaves to the bark is poisonous. You must even be careful of the air you breathe, for it can taint the air as well. Take the gardening gloves and use them to carry back an apple from the tree. When you arrive, I'll show you how to make the antidote, but hurry before you're too late."

"Where can I find the Manchineel tree?"

"The man who gave you the potion is most likely Nightshade. You can find the antidote where you found the potion. It's a tree with pale green apples hanging from its branches. You must take the apple without touching the tree."

"Who's Nightshade?"

"A man who wishes for my demise. He must know that Rose is bound to me. Find the antidote quickly, but be weary if you see him. He's cunning and dangerous. He can change shapes, but he has no whites in his eyes. They are black as night and his hair is slick and black."

"Thank you. I'll be careful," Gabriel said.

He grabbed the gardening gloves from the corner of the greenhouse and raced out the greenhouse door. He quickly detached the small cart from his horse and mounted it. He set off towards the botanist's house on the edge of town at a breakneck pace.

When he arrived, the sun was just peeking over the horizon, and he caught a glimpse of a green apple as he approached. The shadow of a figure hid in the shadows. It was the sinister man from his dreams. No pupils and slick hair. It was Nightshade.

"I see you healed after the tumble you took from your horse," Nightshade said with a smirk.

Gabriel braced himself to fend off this vicious creature, but Nightshade simply looked amused.

"You swindling trickster. That was no potion; that was a poison! If I weren't in such a hurry, I would have your head."

"I'd love to see you try. In the meantime, would you like an apple from the Manchineel tree? There's one right over there, if you can handle it. I'll even let you use my ax," he said and threw an ax that looked like it was meant for a child in Gabriel's general direction. He pointed to the tree bearing green apples and waved Gabriel off.

Gabriel threw a questioning look at Nightshade, but decided not to look this gift horse in the mouth. It was the same tree the woman had described. He rushed over to the tree, barely remembering to slip on his gloves as he approached and chopped off a lone apple. A stray piece of bark hit him on the arm as he cut the apple free, burning his skin, and he brushed it off with his gloved hand. With care, Gabriel slipped the apple in his messenger bag and grabbed his horse. He quickly rode back towards the greenhouse, and as he rode the sun beat down on him.

He dismounted from his horse and pulled open the greenhouse door. There he saw Rose lying on the floor. Her skin was red and dry, her eyes were dilated. She only moved with an occasional involuntary tremor, but otherwise remained still.

"I have retrieved the apple, as you asked," he said to Belladonna.

"Wonderful. Now, kindle the fire for the wood burning stove. You must wash the apple with water, then slice it thin. Be careful that none of the juices touch you. Then you will place it on a tray directly over the heat of the stove until it dries. This will be the antidote to flush out the poison."

He did as the Nymph instructed and felt her gaze focus on him as he started the fire on the stove. He prepared the apple, bathing it in a bucket of water he drew from the garden hose, being careful so as not to be burned once again.

When the fruit was sufficiently dry, he took it off of the stove and brought it over to Rose's gaunt form. He broke the slices into small pieces and opened her mouth, forcing her to swallow the dried apple. She coughed slightly as it slid down her throat.

He looked over at the woman and her gaze had softened. She said tenderly, "The antidote will flush out the poison. You may want her near the washroom for now."

He gingerly lifted her up, cradling her head and carried her to the washroom, then gently placed her in the tub. He clumsily removed any extra layers of clothing and changed her into fresh attire. All the while he kept his gaze averted to give her privacy. Red colored his cheeks as he worked.

For the next several days, he didn't leave her side. Every time she needed water or food, he was there to care for her. Worry crept in as the time passed, *What if this is like Lara, and I truly can't help her,* He thought as he changed the damp washcloth once again. He shook his head to banish the thought. Gluing himself to her side, he continued to change washcloths out until her fever broke. He broke food into small pieces and fed her some small morsels, being careful so she wouldn't choke. He managed to get her to sip at water, half conscious, so she wouldn't dehydrate. The same thought circled in his mind. "She has to be okay," he would say to himself.

As he cared for her, he imagined her resolve and persistence. The flush of her cheeks when his face lingered near hers. He needed her to survive.

He cleaned her and watched over her as her body slowly rid itself of the poison from the treacherous Nightshade.

After several days passed, Gabriel was rewarded with a slight flutter of her eyes. She was able to speak to him, though she could barely move.

"Gabriel? Where am I?" she mumbled.

Tears freely flowed from him, and some spilled from his eyelids and onto Rose. "You're in the greenhouse, Rose. I couldn't help you escape. I'm sorry. If it weren't for Belladonna, you'd be dead."

"It's okay Gabriel. I'm just glad that you're safe," she said and reached her hand up over the edge of the tub to cup his cheek with her palm. "But who is Belladonna?"

"She's a nymph who gave your mother a potion, so she could give birth to you,"

"I suppose I owe her a thank you, then."

"Maybe we both do." He straightened his back and ruffled his hair with one hand, the other hand toyed with his sleeve. "Rose, you almost died being so reckless. Please don't ever do something like that again."

CHAPTER 31

Gabriel had burn marks on several parts of his skin, and the dark rings under his eyes showed a lack of sleep. His forehead showed telltale creases of worry.

"Shouldn't I be saying that to you? Look at the burns on your skin. What did you do, stick your arms into the oven?" Rose joked.

His sheepish grin told her that he'd either done exactly that or something equally dangerous.

"Gabriel. You looked exhausted. Maybe now it's your turn to rest? I've had several days of that."

She heard him mutter, "It's called a coma, not rest." He gave her hand one brief squeeze before he exited the tiny washroom and went to her small bed to get some rest.

A woman appeared. Her eyes were the same green as a plant's vines and she was clad in greenery. "Are you Belladonna?" Rose asked.

"Yes, I am," she said. "Rose, that man watched over you the whole time. He nursed you back to health when you were poisoned. He cares deeply for you. Do you care for him?" It was the same voice from Rose's thoughts.

"I care for him, but how can I be with him if I can never leave this place?"

The white roses turned silver as Belladonna fully materialized. She plucked a silver rose from the ground and beckoned for Rose to come over.

"Come here my child," Belladonna said.

Rose dazedly headed towards her. She moved ever closer, and Belladonna handed her the silver rose. She leaned down and whispered in Rose's ear, "Steep the petals of this rose and you will be able to leave."

Immediately Rose's jaw dropped in shock. "H-h-how? Why?" Rose asked.

"Rose. I'm sorry. You were bound here by me for your protection. Your mother couldn't have children, so she'd asked me for assistance. I brewed her a potion of roses that would allow her to bear a child. As part of the bargain, you were only allowed to be in the greenhouse or your house. When you were born, your mother broke the bargain with me and tried to flee town with you, and, as punishment, you couldn't leave the greenhouse for extended periods of time otherwise you'd become severely ill and die. It was meant to punish her. I'd never imagined it would cause you such suffering."

Her face crumpled, and silent tears trickled down her cheeks. "I almost lost you from my own selfishness, but now I want to set you free. Please go and take the man with you," she wiped the tears from her face and composed herself.

In a warning tone, she said, "But, Rose, be wary of other Nymphs as they may seek your destruction.. Nightshade, a nymph with only darkness in his eyes wants both of us dead. You will have to move quickly to stay safe. Don't linger in one place for too long."

Happiness and anger momentarily warred within her. Her face lit up with an earnest smile despite the warning, and she padded over to where Gabriel had gone to rest.

She practically pounced on his sleeping form until he said a groggy, "Yes, Rose?"

CHAPTER 32

Gabriel was curious as to what was going on and leveled a questioning look at Rose.

"She said we can leave! I just have to drink tea with this," Rose said waving around a silver rose.

Rose must have realized the questioning look on Gabriel's face because she said, "She's the reason I couldn't leave before. I was bound by a bargain of sorts, but she's willing to release me. I'll answer more questions later. For now, we should leave quickly. We just have to steep the rose petals first. Can you do it?" She shoved the rose at him and then rushed off without waiting for an answer.

Gabriel kindled a fire for the oven then found a small steel kettle, filled it with water and put it on to boil. "We're finally free."

A happy sigh escaped his lips, and his mind wandered to thoughts of them together in his home. She would wake him up with a light kiss, and they'd travel from town to town together, arm in arm. He was pulled from his daydreaming by the whistling of the kettle as the water came to a boil.

After Rose drank the tea, she wandered out of Gabriel's sight for a moment, and when she returned, she had a knapsack that contained the mirror, and if he saw it correctly, some clothing. She began tugging Gabriel out of the greenhouse.

He briefly gazed at the forest-eyed woman trying to grasp his current situation, then decided he didn't want to know for now and let Rose pull him out to the carriage. They got in and headed back to his home.

Chapter 33

Once they entered the house, Gabriel turned and surveyed the forest surrounding his home. Satisfied danger wasn't currently lurking in the shadows, he locked the door and turned to Rose.

"Okay, Rose, we're safe for now. Please tell me exactly what happened."

With his hand on the small of her back, Gabriel urged her over to the sofa. He sat beside her, angling his body to give her his full attention. He still wasn't certain she wouldn't get sick away from the white roses. Gabriel planned to watch her carefully in case he had to rush her back to keep her safe.

Rose nervously tucked her hair behind her ear.

"My mother entered into a contract with this strange woman named Belladonna. Part of the deal was that I wasn't allowed to leave the greenhouse for long periods of time. If I did, I'd become seriously ill. If I stayed away for too long, I'd die. Well, when I was born, my mother tried to flee town with me, so as punishment to my mother, I was cursed to live the rest of my life in the greenhouse. That's why my mother tried to keep me from escaping."

Rose paused for a moment to let Gabriel take this all in.

"When she saw how you cared for me, she entrusted me to you and set me free. She also warned that we would need to flee. There are other dangers out there, a man named Nightshade, and other Nymphs that want to hurt me because of my bond with Belladonna."

When she'd finished telling the tale, Gabriel had several unanswered question, but frankly he was afraid of what the answers to his questions would be, so he kept his mouth shut.

His mind thought, *Who is this woman? Why does she have so much power over Rose? How do we know we can trust her? Why would she trust me with Rose? Why did she wait until now to break the bargain?*

These were mere side questions compared to the one currently screaming with urgency to be answered. *What other dangers?*

Gabriel tried to brush away the questions beating away at his mind. He needed to stay composed, so he could get answers without seeming too desperate for information. He started off slowly, asking the most important question at the moment, "How shall we keep you safe?"

"We must lie low and never stay in one place too long. You may have to rebuild your life. If you do not wish this, then I may continue on my own."

"I shall do what is necessary. I do not have much of a life here anymore."

"Then we shall leave in the morning," Rose said.

They both headed to separate bedrooms for the night. Rose took one short glance at Gabriel's retreating form before swinging open the door to her bedroom. She knew she would not sleep well this night because what the woman had said was still running through her mind.

She sat on the edge of the bed and wondered if her stories were true. *Had her mother been infertile? Did this strange woman help create her?*

Chapter 34

Gabriel couldn't sleep. Unanswered questions circuited through his mind like his daily deliveries, unending and never changing. How was he supposed to protect her when he was most likely her greatest threat? No matter where they went, he felt certain that Nightshade would follow them, torment him, and try to injure Rose.

The scene from his meeting with Nightshade circled his mind. Nightshade had mentioned his fall off the horse. He had a sudden realization. Nightshade was the reason he hadn't been able to get back to Rose for months, the reason his leg had almost been amputated. The thought sent a shiver down his spine.

Remaining close to Rose was putting her in great danger, but he couldn't bring himself to leave. He felt drawn to her; he wanted, needed, to be by her side, but frantic worries vied for attention in his mind, *What will I do when Nightshade comes after me? How will Rose react if she realizes that I made a deal with Nightshade for that poison? Would she leave me? Hate me?*

Gabriel whispered his biggest fear to himself, "I still don't know what favor Nightshade wants for that potion. What if he asks me to kill her? What will happen if I refuse his request?" Gabriel whispered to himself.

He feared both Rose's reaction and the reaction of the woman with the forest eyes.

CHAPTER 35

After several hours of lying in bed and staring at the ceiling, Rose finally drifted off to sleep, but her dreams assured she didn't get a good night's rest. The nightmare was vague this time. The dream was shrouded in darkness and through the darkness she heard a sinister voice, a man's voice, *"I hope you enjoy your freedom. It will be the death of you."* After that, she only saw fragments: a flash of Gabriel's emerald eyes, a potion, the words *a deal* spoken by the dark man, and a mirror like the one from Gabriel, only shattered. A figure moved closer to her through the darkness, and the voice grew louder, more frightening, until it jolted her awake. The darkness in the sky was still full-fledged. She wondered whether this dream held some truth as the one with the forest eyed woman had.

She crept across the hall until she reached the door to Gabriel's bedroom.

Perhaps I can convince him to leave early if he is awake as well, Rose thought.

She cracked open the door and saw Gabriel's silhouette lying on the bed motionless. Rose moved closer to make sure he was still sleeping and was startled when he bolted upright in bed. For a few moments he seemed disoriented. Then his eyes focused on Rose,

"Another nightmare?" Gabriel asked groggily.

"It appears that you also awoke with a start."

Gabriel didn't respond to this. Instead, he patted the side of the bed as an invitation, and she sat down but didn't surrender herself to the mattress even though it was much softer than her usual fare.

For several moments, she just perched herself on the edge of the bed, unwilling to submit to the comfort of the mattress despite her tired state. It wasn't until she turned around and he gave her one of his signature smirks that she shrugged her shoulders in defeat and swung herself the rest of the way onto the bed. She immediately fell into a deep sleep.

When Rose finally awoke again, the gray light of dawn was streaming through the window. Gabriel lay beside her his breathing deep and even. He was still asleep. She slipped out of bed, and headed to her room to get dressed, and began preparing for their leave. Rose leafed through her dresser, rummaging through some drawers until she found a perfectly-sized bag with a leather strap on it. Then, she tiptoed her way to the kitchen and began looking for any food that could be easily carried, and would keep. She packed some bread, dried fruit, and nuts for food, then moved on to find something that would help start a fire and found some matches which she quickly threw into the sack.

She continued to forage for their journey until the sun was almost completely dominant in the sky, and Rose was finally confident she'd packed all the provisions they'd need for their journey to different areas.

She was nervous and thrilled at the thought of this new adventure. Rose had just put the bag to the side and had begun making breakfast when Gabriel walked into the kitchen. The smell of eggs coated the air. She'd been using up some perishables in the house by making omelets for breakfast and serving them with two glasses of milk, one for each of them.

"I suppose I am now the guest, seeing as you're the one making breakfast?" Gabriel said playfully.

"I was simply showing you some kindness considering you're housing me," Rose said giving him a mocking smile.

At this, Gabriel simply shrugged his shoulders and went to sit down at the kitchen table.

"Wow, the eggs are only burnt in the center. Amazing," He said sarcastically as they ate and she elbowed him. After that, she glared over at Gabriel anytime he'd smirk and open his mouth to say something.

"Stop talking," she said.

He deflated and his grin turned into a smile, "I didn't say anything yet,"

"You didn't have to." After that, they ate without Gabriel making any more jabs at Rose's cooking, and as Gabriel went to get the horse ready, Rose grabbed her supplies and the mirror Gabriel had given her. She headed out to see him finishing up with the horse and said, "Where are we traveling?"

"We will be going to a place a few towns over. The doctor had hired me as a courier there when I had been injured. Perhaps, I will be able to regain that job once we arrive. For now, we will be riding to a town about a day's ride from here and rest at an inn."

Rose jumped into the carriage and settled into the small compartment. Gabriel mounted the horse, and they set off at a miserably slow pace to the next town. After a few hours, Rose began asking Gabriel random questions just for the sake of passing time.

"What's your favorite color?"

"Blue," he replied flatly.

"Hmm. How old are you?"

"22," He said flatly, again.

Rose eyes widened and she gasped, "Really?"

"You're that surprised?" Gabriel said to her eyebrow raised questioningly.

"I thought you were old," she said.

"Are you calling me old?" he said with a joking smile.

At that, Rose pursed her lips and then said, "Why did you become a courier?"

"Changing the topic, huh? It was the first job I could find," he said with a slight laugh and a shrug.

The conversation was going well until she asked him, "Whose bedroom is it, the one you let me stay in, and what happened to her?"

Gabriel stiffened at the question, as if her asking the question caused him physical pain, and then he took a deep breath, which seemed to relax him enough to say, "She died."

"Who was she? How did she die? Why did she have her own room?" Rose asked, but was answered only with the pounding of the horse's hooves on the dirt road.

When they arrived in the town, Rose guessed that he was still giving her the silent treatment. He led the horse into a small stable and undid it from the carriage and its harness, then walked over to the inn's entrance with Rose in tow. She was still convinced he was done talking to her for now when he leaned into her ear and said, "We'll need to pretend we're married; otherwise, the innkeeper will not allow us to sleep in the same room."

"Well, maybe I'd prefer a separate room."

Gabriel raised his eyebrows at Rose in a brief look of disbelief, then said, "Maybe you would, but I know you can't afford it, and neither can I."

Rose reluctantly agreed to his terms. When they reached the check in desk the innkeeper said to them, "Do you need rooms for tonight? We have two single rooms left."

"We shall only need one room for the both of us as we just recently married."

Yes, sure we're married… as of ten seconds ago when Gabriel decided we couldn't afford a second room, thought Rose.

She nearly burst out laughing. Gabriel seemed to notice and remedied it with a surprise kiss on her lips. Her eyes widened, and she made a note to give him trouble for that sneak attack later. She touched a hand to her lips. Her first kiss. *How dare he and after ignoring me the whole way here. What's wrong with him?* Rose thought.

However absurd the statement and sudden kiss was to Rose, it fooled the innkeeper enough to let them share a single room for the night.

As soon as they entered the room, Rose whirled on him and said, "What's the big idea kissing me like that? That was my first kiss, you know. Do you have anything to say for yourself?"

"Gabriel's eyes widened; his cheeks reddened briefly, and he turned his face away in an attempt to hide it, "I'm sorry. I didn't realize. I was just trying to make it convincing, and you looked like you were about to laugh." It wasn't easy for me, either. You're a lot like her," he said sadly.

"Who is her?"

"No one. Stop asking me," he snapped.

She stepped back a few paces when he raised his voice. The image of her father with a metal wire flashed through her mind and she shook her head to clear her mind. She was shaking.

"W-w-ell, I suppose we should go to sleep for now, the sun is beginning to set, but I'm not sleeping near you and you're not watching me change," she said and puffed out her chest and turned her nose up at him.

He lifted his hands up, feigning innocence and smiled before turning around so she could change. Rose grabbed a dressing gown that was hanging in the closet and switched her clothing, looking back frequently to make sure he wasn't peeking.

When they went down to rest, Rose put a pillow between them and said, "If you try to kiss me again, you'll be sleeping at the bottom of a river," before turning her back away from him.

With a slight mumble he said, "I wouldn't dream of it." They slept turned away from each other and when they awoke the sun had risen, and they were both well rested.

CHAPTER 36

Gabriel's first thought that morning was that he didn't like lying to her. He could've afforded the separate room, but he didn't want her alone with who-knows-what creatures after her. It could have been dangerous.

Before they left, Rose turned to him and asked, "Who was it that lived in that room?"

Gabriel stiffened again, but then he had an idea of how he could get her to drop the topic and he grinned. He turned towards her and said mockingly, "Why? Are you jealous of her?"

At this Rose huffed. "Sorry I asked," she said then stormed out of their room.

Gabriel followed her, rolling his eyes at her dramatic response. *Typical Rose,* he thought.

When he reached the inn entrance, he saw a ruffled Rose and continued on past her to ready the horse. The innkeeper's expression was amused, as if to ask Gabriel, *Lover's quarrel?*

Gabriel brought the horse around to the front of the inn, then watched as Rose approached the carriage still looking irritated as ever. The ride to the next town was filled with only the sound of hoof beats. Whenever he looked back to check on her, he was met with a death glare.

They reached the next stop on their journey just as the sun was beginning to set. This time she refused to share a room. Instead, he settled for two rooms directly next to each other. With Rose still mad at him and in another room, the night was mostly silent. That is, until he began to hear the man's voice in his head again. Only this time, when he heard the voice he was still awake.

"She must be destroyed," said the voice.

"Who?" Gabriel asked.

"The woman with the forest eyes."

Then the voice disappeared, and Gabriel was left alone with his thoughts. He was still awake when the sound of Rose tossing and mumbling echoed through the thin walls. It seemed she was having another nightmare. He grabbed the spare key and walked to the room next door. He let himself in and went over to her bed, sat down next to her, and began to stroke her hair, saying meaningless words to soothe her restless form. Eventually, her breathing became even as she began to calm back down, but Gabriel still sat there until he began to feel himself tire. He then went to his own bed to fall asleep.

When he woke up, the sun was shining bright on his face, and Rose was staring down at him as if he were dead and she was wondering what to do with the body. When she recognized he was awake, she started a little then said, "Look who's back among the living." Rose said.

"Look who decided to break her vow of silence," Gabriel replied.

"Well, I suppose I can't stay mad at you forever...even if you stubbornly refuse to admit who that woman was," She said gaze averted and reached for his hand.

He grabbed her outstretched hand absentmindedly. "Maybe sometime soon, but not just yet," he said. His gaze focused somewhere far away. She thought he looked sad for a moment, but just as quickly as the sadness was there, he had hidden it away again.

He brightly exclaimed, "Are you ready to leave?"

Rose dropped his gaze for a moment then looked up and said, "I had a frightening dream."

"What was it about?" Gabriel asked and squeezed her hand a little tighter.

"The scenery was dark. A man with flat black eyes appeared and said, with a devilish smile, that I was going to die and that you were going to kill me. Then, Belladonna appeared and told me to run. The man told her to stay out of it. He held out his hand and she flinched in pain. When she was in pain, I could feel it, but it was a dull pain, not like what she felt. Then, you were there murmuring things saying it was going to be okay. The man called you a fool. He said you would regret it. Then, he disappeared."

For a moment, Gabriel just sat and let what she'd said sink in. The part that worried him the most was the threat to himself, to make him pay for what he'd done. Perhaps, for not doing the favor for Nightshade, although he still wasn't sure what the menacing man wanted from him.

Gabriel pulled Rose to him. He embraced her and said, "I won't let anything happen to you, Rose." He wasn't sure how he'd keep that promise.

It was that precise moment that Rose broke the serious moment with a sarcastic remark, "Other than when you annoy me to death?"

Gabriel and Rose started laughing at the same time and when they both managed to stop they packed up and headed out for the next village. *As they left, Gabriel thought he saw Lara off in the distance, but when he shook his head in surprise she'd disappeared.*

CHAPTER 37

The outline of a hospital appeared on the horizon as the sun began to set.

"We're going to make a quick stop before we go find a place to stay for the night," Gabriel said.

When the hospital started to come into view, Rose murmured a string of half-finished curses and protests. She wasn't about to go to another hospital after her experience at the last one. Gabriel looked back at her panic-stricken face and added.

"He's a former employer. I'm just here to ask him about employment."

At that, Rose relaxed slightly. *We aren't here for me. Good*, she thought.

"What work did you do in this town?"

"I was a courier."

"Is it a job you like?"

"It's a job I'm good at," he said.

Rose was glad he wasn't working as medical staff. She sighed in relief and kept silent as Gabriel tied up the horse and walked into the doctor's office. She followed just a few paces behind him, watching as he approached a doctor. After getting directions to find the doctor Gabriel knew, they headed down a long corridor.

Rose marveled at the size of the facility. They passed room after room. Her experience with hospitals was limited to the one visit, but in comparison, this place was massive. They went down a few corridors until they reached a sterile looking room. The walls were painted snow-white, and all the furniture matched the color of the wall.

The man who approached them was wearing white linen pants, a blue button up shirt with a stiff collar, and a butcher's apron, most likely to keep blood off of his clothing. Rose watched as the doctor took one look at Gabriel, then one long look at her. When he spoke to Gabriel his tone was serious, but his words were teasing.

"I see you found that girl you were so desperate to get back to. Was it worth it?"

"If it weren't, would she be with me right now?" Gabriel said and flashed him a devilish grin.

Whenever Gabriel didn't want to answer something, he always deflected by answering with a question. He'd already done it to Rose on several occasions during the time they'd known each other. She shrugged her shoulders, resigned. She supposed that was part of his charm, even if it could get annoying. His answer seemed to satisfy the doctor's curiosity.

"I suppose that's true," The doctor said, then paused. "What brings you back to this town? Are you in need of more work or just looking for a new place for yourself and your lover?"

"Just the former…unless the lady would approve of the title of lover?" He turned and raised an eyebrow at her.

"Don't get your hopes up just yet." Rose piped up.

"You haven't yet snared her with your wicked ways?" the doctor asked.

"Alas, I have not done so yet," He said with an exaggerated sigh and she saw the corner of a grin on his face.

Then, Gabriel feigned a cough and said "Back to business. Do you need another courier or must I wander to another town in search of work?"

"I have work for you Gabriel, and I have work for the lady as well, if need be."

"We shall see," Gabriel said.

"Very well then. Just follow me, and I'll get you set up with some deliveries."

They followed the doctor back to the lobby, and he disappeared through a door behind the front desk. When he came out, he held a brown sack that was filled to the brim with letters from patients and, probably, some medicine.

"I'd been having some nurses do the mail runs, but the office has been so busy lately that even they have been unable to help."

"Thank you for the help, Doctor. Do you know where to find the nearest lodgings?"

"There's a nice inn across the way. They need a few more hands to help run the inn if the lady is interested in a job."

Rose had her fill of being called the lady, today "My name is Rose. If it isn't too much of a burden, please do use it,"

The doctor chuckled good-naturedly and said, "Then, Rose it is. Her words even have the prick of a rose's thorns." She was fairly sure anyone else would've been insulted by her biting comment.

"Well, I'm off to work," Gabriel said.

Then, with a motion that seemed effortless, he flipped the sack over his shoulder and walked out to his horse without another word. Rose took one moment to stare, mouth agape, at his somewhat abrupt exit then muttered a quick *sorry* to the doctor before exiting the hospital.

Rose walked to the inn across the street. At the front desk was a young-looking blonde girl with blue eyes. When she saw Rose, she searched the surrounding space.

Then, looking confused, she inquired, "Do you have a traveling companion? Are you looking for a room?"

"Yes, but he's working. May, I book the room?" Rose asked, her gaze pleading.

The woman's gaze was thoughtful for a moment. She said, "Sure. What's your companion's name?"

"Gabriel," Rose chimed. Then she said sheepishly, "I also wanted to know if you require any work at this inn."

"We require another innkeeper. Would you like to apply for the job?" She asked in a voice that resembled a songbird.

"Yes," Rose said with a beaming smile.

"One moment, please, while I fetch the owner."

The blonde retreated from the front desk and scampered up the staircase. After a few minutes, she came back with what appeared to be an older version of herself. Rose guessed this was the girl's mother.

"This is the girl you wanted to hire? Do you even know this young lady's name?" the older woman asked.

"No, Mother. I'm afraid I forgot, again," she said timidly. Her eyes were focused on the ground.

"Why don't you ask her?" the older woman chided.

"Pardon me, but I forgot to ask your name. What—?"

"My name is Rose," Rose said stopping her mid-sentence.

"Well, she seems lacking in manners, but that could be fixed, and we do need some more hands to run the inn… Fine, she's hired, but she's your responsibility. She has a week to impress me. If she does, she can stay. If not, she will be fired. Understood?"

"Yes, Mother," she said sternly. She seemed to bubble with excitement at the prospect of Rose working there, though Rose didn't quite understand why. The girl's mother walked away and Rose wondered why the girl would be so happy.

She'd never interacted with anyone other than her mother when she'd been in the greenhouse, and frankly, even that interaction was limited. It wasn't until she met Gabriel that she'd ever been around other people at length and the only other woman she'd met had been the innkeeper a few towns back, when they'd lied to her telling them that they were married.

She supposed this girl was looking forward to the company of someone other than her mother. Now that she thought of it, it was understandable to Rose, considering she'd run away from home because she couldn't bear the confinement and the loneliness of the greenhouse any longer.

With that on her mind, Rose said, "I'm willing to learn what you have to teach me about working here," and matched the girl's sunshine smile with a sly smile of her own.

CHAPTER 38

Gabriel could not have left the doctor's office faster. The moment the doctor mentioned the possible job at the inn, Gabriel's thoughts shifted to Lara, and his fear that Rose would follow in her footsteps bubbled to the surface. He felt a painful squeeze in his heart at the thought of losing her. If she left, he would shatter once again. He felt like he was suffocating in that office, so he rushed out to get some air and clear his thoughts.

When the breeze ruffled his clothes and the fresh air filled his lungs, he relaxed slightly. The busy route the doctor had assigned him kept some of his worries at bay. He rushed to finish the deliveries before sundown because there were very few gaslights in this town. When he delivered the last package, the sky grew dark. The route he'd taken had landed him on the side of town, so his ride back to the inn was only lit by the din of some gaslights. Gabriel headed to the stables near the inn and unhitched his horse from the mail carrier. Then, he handed off his horse to the stable hand so it could be put away for the night.

When Gabriel entered the inn he heard a cheery voice say, "Welcome to Ivy Inn. How may I help you?" and for a moment he was relieved that she hadn't taken the job when he saw a blonde woman manning the desk. But when he approached the desk, he caught a glimpse of Rose's red eyes and nearly walked right back out of the hotel to escape this nightmare turned reality. *It's happening again*, He thought.

"I'd like to reserve a room for the night. That is, unless Rose here has taken care of that already?"

The blonde looked at her expectantly, but Rose just blinked at Gabriel as if to say "who me?" then said, "I'm not certain who you are sir, but I will gladly put you up for the night. We have plenty of rooms."

Gabriel gave Rose a disbelieving look and said "Very funny. Now tell the nice young lady working with you that we're traveling together and that you're pretending you don't know me because it amuses you."

"Whatever could you mean sir? I've never met you before a day in my life," Rose said with a bat of her eyelashes and a small giggle, giving the charade away to the girl working with her.

The blonde let out a small laugh and said to Gabriel, "Rose reserved a room earlier today, but I didn't realize you were the traveling companion she'd mentioned. I apologize for the inconvenience, and I'll fetch you your room key now." She turned around to face the array of keys behind the desk and plucked one from its cubby hole, then turned to Gabriel and plopped it into his open palm.

"Please enjoy your stay," The girl chirped, but she might as well have been saying it to a wall, because the second Gabriel received the key he bolted out of the lobby and practically ran up the stairs to where the rooms were.

When he reached the top of the stairway, he looked at the number on his key and then skimmed the numbers on the rooms until he found room 113. He retreated into his quarters and shut the door behind him just as another wave of emotion seized him. He choked back tears at the thought of Rose sick, unmoving.

He thought of Lara and the terrible end that had befallen her. Seeing Rose working the same job that Lara had before she died, this was too much to bear. In his mind, Lara's face morphed and became Rose. Thoughts of Rose facing an equally terrible demise washed over his mind like a tidal wave and sobs racked his body. Tears streamed down his face.

He decided he couldn't let Nightshade win. No matter what that wretched Nymph asked, he wouldn't comply. He had to keep his Rose safe at any cost.

CHAPTER 39

After Gabriel left in a rush, Rose's new coworker turned to her and said, "What's your relation to your traveling companion? Are you siblings, friends, or something more?" The girl emphasized "something more" by raising her eyebrows at Rose.

Rose shrugged at the question and said, "I wouldn't consider us lovers and we aren't siblings, but I'm not entirely sure I'd consider us just friends, either. We're somewhere in between friends and lovers, I suppose?"

She said it with conviction, but then Rose's mind wandered off to how he'd kissed her at the previous inn, how he'd watched over her when she'd been poisoned, and how he often held her hand. The thought of his lips on hers sent blood rushing to her face and she covered her cheeks with her hands. *I wish he'd kiss me for real*, Rose thought with a sigh.

She must have caught her blushing because the girl said, "Ah! So you ARE lovers. It's a darn shame. I thought he was rather handsome, but as long as he's happy with you, I suppose I can let this one go," the girl said with a wink and a shrug.

They continued to chat like this, until an old man with a permanent frown walked in and the blonde girl commented, "That man is the local grouser. He always has something to complain about." Sure enough, a little while later, he came up to complain about how the light in his room was too bright and they giggled together after he'd left. When a group of women walked in, dressed in beautiful dresses of bright greens, yellows, and oranges, she'd turned to Rose and said, "Why are they all gussied up?" Eventually, the girl grew tired of commenting on the patrons and focused on Rose.

"Where are you planning to travel?" the girl asked.

"Well, right now we're just wandering from place to place. I haven't seen much of the world, so I hope we can go all around the country," Rose said.

Her eyes lit up just thinking of an adventure across the country and her thoughts wandered off to leisurely travels with Gabriel as the girl talked about where she would want to travel. When Rose heard the girl's chatter stop, she turned to look at what had caught her eye and spotted several men dressed in full suits. They wore colorful shirts with stiff collars and plain striped slacks. Even their shoes were dark, well-polished leather and several of them wore a full suit jacket.

The girl elbowed Rose and said, "So, which one do you fancy?"

Rose initially would have shrugged and said "none", but after a while of being prodded, she realized it was easier to go along with the charade and would point to one at random and say "him." Her coworker remained unconvinced that she wasn't Gabriel's lover, but she included Rose, inviting her to ogle some younger male guests.

The conversation was dull at times, but Rose was glad for it. It kept her mind off the jealousy she felt towards this woman that Gabriel refused to talk about. It distracted her from being haunted by the black, soulless eyes of the evil thing that caused them to flee town.

In fact, the time had passed so fast that Rose was surprised when the sun was starting to come up at the end of her first shift. She dismissed Rose from the desk and continued on working in her ever-energetic and cheerful way while Rose yawned and headed to the room to get some sleep.

Rose headed to room 113. When she found the door locked, she reached her hand out to knock and almost hit Gabriel's chest instead when he suddenly opened the door. His hair was tousled from sleep, but he still looked tired, like he'd tossed and turned the entire night. His eyes were bloodshot and looked lifeless and glassy.

He ran his hand through his golden brown hair, then sidestepped Rose and rushed off without a word.

Rose wanted to make some sarcastic remark about his unusual behavior, but when she went to open her mouth she just sputtered and stopped. She had no comments, criticisms or comebacks. Any other form of retort died when she saw the sadness and anger lurking in his eyes. Rose had truly been stunned silent.

She held the door open mechanically as she recovered from the tense moment and the whirlwind of emotions that Gabriel had subjected her to as he'd walked past. When she finally recovered, she let herself inside, plopped herself down on the closest bed, and quickly fell into a deep sleep.

CHAPTER 40

Gabriel had barely slept because every time he'd closed his eyes he'd seen Nightshade. He could still hear the dark voice in his mind that was as slick as oil.

Nightshade was in the forest where they'd first met. He cupped Belladonna's cheek, kissing her. Then Gabriel saw the sinister man break her neck with ease and let her body drop to the floor. He shuddered. Nightshade was dressed in an all-black suit, like at a funeral.

Destroy Belladonna and I'll leave you and Rose alone for good. Deny me and I'll kill them both.

Why should I trust you? You already tried to trick me once.

Gabriel thought he saw anger blaze in his eyes briefly, but then his lips curved with a lazy smile, and he said, *The nature spirit is worth a hundred of Rose. I have a debt to settle with you. Poison or not, you used the potion, so now you owe me a favor. If you want to fulfill it, then kill her.*

After that, he'd disappeared. Nightshade hadn't asked for an immediate answer, but he'd kill Rose if Gabriel didn't answer soon. Gabriel didn't know how to answer. He thought, *Could I ever go through with killing someone even if she isn't human? What would happen if I killed Belladonna? Would she reinstate the curse on Rose when she realized that I couldn't be trusted? Would I even be able to destroy such a creature? Will he even keep the bargain this time or just ask me to kill even more? Is there a way out of this? What misfortune will befall me if I don't do it?* The same questions kept going through his mind. If he didn't distract himself soon, he'd do something he'd regret.

When he opened the door, Rose was in the doorway. *He saw Nightshade behind her grabbing her neck* and, in a panic, he shoved

Nightshade away and ran. He had to get out of there now, away from Rose. If Nightshade could now toy with his waking mind, there was no telling what he could do.

Gabriel hooked his horse up to his carriage, then set out to the hospital for his daily mail run. As he got farther away, shame engulfed him. He remembered how he'd rudely shoved Rose, and he wondered if she'd think he was angry at her. As he went along his mail route, the same questions looped through his mind. Each time he considered harming Belladonna, he became more disgusted with himself. Rationalizing murder wasn't like him. When his work was done, he was no closer to forming a plan. His anger and frustration were bubbling to the surface when he arrived back at the inn.

CHAPTER 41

"You need to get away. You're in danger."

"What danger?" Rose asked the nature spirit's voice.

"Someone you trust is working for him… Nightshade."

"Who wants to harm me?" Rose didn't know much about Nightshade, but hearing his name sent shivers down her spine.

Her questions were answered with dead silence. Rose awoke to the lazy afternoon sun and the sound of someone knocking on the door. Rose thought it was Gabriel and was going to ignore him, but then she realized Gabriel had the key; he didn't need to knock. Wearily, Rose crept to the room's entrance and opened the door enough to see bright blonde hair. She realized it was nearly time for her shift and that the person at the door was definitely not Gabriel. Rose opened the door the rest of the way and was met with a whirlwind of energy.

"Rose! Are you about ready? I have more to teach you about your job today."

"We aren't working at the desk?" Rose asked.

"Today, we're working on customer service. We provide meals for all of our guests, so our job right now is going to be to go to everyone's room and ask if they'd like to go downstairs for dinner."

"That sounds simple enough," Rose said.

The girl smiled her sugar-sweet smile, but Rose swore she could see a hint of mischief in it this time when she said, "Then let's get started."

By the time they were done, Rose thought her face was going to fall off from forcing on a smile for too long. Her legs ached from running from room to room. After greeting the guests, they'd also had to help serve dinner and clean up the plates and silverware. All the while the girl was smiling and laughing openly as Rose struggled to stay on her feet.

Just as they'd finished cleaning up the last of the dishes from dinner, the hotel door had swung open and, as cheerily as always, the blonde girl rushed to the desk so she could greet them as they entered.

Rose followed her to the desk and Gabriel walked into the hotel. His face looked worn in the fleeing daylight as if he were in his early thirties rather than a young man only six years her senior. The more time Rose spent with him, the older he seemed. It was as if his past had aged him prematurely.

"Hi Gabriel," Rose said as Gabriel paced past the desk.

When Gabriel finally responded, there was no lightness to his tone and his gaze was distant and detached. He didn't look at her when he said, "Hi Rose," then stomped off to their room. His expression was closed off.

Rose turned to her coworker, who gave Rose a "go ahead" look. Rose trotted off behind him and reached the room just in time to catch the door as he slammed it. It barely missed whacking her in the face. Gabriel whirled around when he heard the thwack.

"Shouldn't you be working?" Gabriel said, with a spike of venom to his voice.

Rose opened her mouth to retaliate, but Gabriel's gaze stopped her. He looked conflicted.

"Gabriel, are you unwell?"

"I guess you could say that." He laughed, but the sound held no humor in it.

"What do mean?" Rose choked as her voice caught. She'd never seen him like this, and it tore at her.

At her choked-up form, she saw him momentarily revert to the Gabriel to whom she'd become accustomed. An expression of concern crossed over his features, but the expression merely flickered across his face. Then, it was the empty harsh tempered Gabriel again.

"Go back to work, Rose. I need to be alone right now," he said flatly.

Rose just glanced at him in a daze. If he wanted to be alone, then fine. If he didn't need her, she'd keep far away from him. Rose gathered up her few possessions then headed for the door.

"Where are you going, Rose?" She heard phantom concern in his voice.

"Far away from you!" Rose yelled, slamming the door behind her.

By the time Rose got back to the desk, her bravado had faded and now she was just tired and upset. Rose's coworker caught one glimpse of her then said, "Going somewhere?"

"Yes, as a matter of fact. I need another room just for me."

Her coworker's mouth opened into an O, and she said, "Your traveling partner not so agreeable anymore?"

"I guess you could say that."

The girl rushed to the cubby holes where the keys were kept and grabbed one for her.

"Here's a room as far away from Gabriel as I can get you," she said with a giggle.

"Thanks… I just realized I never asked your name," Rose said with a blush. She was embarrassed that she'd never asked.

"It's April," She said cheerily.

"You're named after a month?" Her brows pulled together in confusion.

"No, it's a family name," April rolled her eyes and busied herself with organizing some room keys.

"Your family is named after a month?" she said with her mouth agape in surprise.

April laughed good-naturedly and Rose knew that was going to be the end of the discussion.

"Here's the key to your new room, Rose." April handed Rose the key to her new room then gave her a shooing motion and said, "Now, off with you."

"What about tonight?" Rose asked.

"Since you worked this afternoon, you won't be working tonight."

With that, Rose scurried to her room, which was only about three rooms away from her previous room. "Oh, so that's how it's going to be," Rose thought as she opened the door to the room. With a sigh of exhaustion, she plopped down on the bed and was asleep almost instantly.

CHAPTER 42

Gabriel paced the room so intensely that anyone watching him would think he was trying to tread a hole into the floor. He hated pushing Rose away, but he didn't know how to help her. He couldn't think or sleep, and now he'd snapped at her. His heart ached for her, but maybe he needed to distance himself. He couldn't come up with a plan, so it was either kill or lose her. The thought of Nightshade wrapping his arms around Rose's neck sent shivers down his spine. His urge to protect her overwhelmed his moral compass. The temptation of Nightshade's offer was too much.

"What's wrong with me? Why did I push her away?" he said to himself.

Another version of him appeared before him. This one was feverish. He rubbed his eyes in confusion, but the image didn't dissipate, and it said, "It's good she left. This way you won't do anything you might regret."

He said to his mirror self, "There has to be some string attached to this bargain. I can't trust him after being tricked with his poison. I have to protect Rose, but I don't want to become a murderer." Gabriel was now talking to himself, literally. His eyes were getting dark circles under them from lack of sleep. Maybe, he was hallucinating from so many sleepless nights. "Go away," he said to his other self.

Then he plopped into bed and went to sleep.

CHAPTER 43

Rose woke up to the sun streaming in the window. It was nearly mid-day. Her first thoughts were of Gabriel's strange behavior last night. She wanted to feel upset or angry, but all she could feel was relief. He'd been acting strange, and she needed a break from his odd behavior. After a stretch and a lazy yawn, Rose hopped out of bed and went to clean up in the washroom, then got dressed for work.

Rose approached the desk to find April beaming at her as she always did. "How long have you been awake?" Rose asked.

"Oh, my mother took over the early morning shift, so I got a good six hours of sleep or so," she said.

She's like a rabbit with all this energy, Rose thought.

Her coworker gave her a sly smile that didn't fit her face and said, "So…do you like your new room?"

"Well, quite frankly, I believe your idea and my idea of far away are vastly different."

"If you'd like to get away from the moping man, perhaps you'd like to come with me to the market today. I need to get some food for the inn."

"Of course, I'd love to join you…if there isn't a catch."

At this, April giggled.

"Of course not. I just wanted some company on my daily errands. My mother will be running the desk until we get back."

"I guess I can go then…" Rose said giving April a distrustful look.

"Okay, I shall go tell my mother. Watch the desk for me until I return," April said with an airy laugh and then disappeared up the stairs.

Rose took care of all the hotel guests checking in and out for the next couple of hours, making polite conversation with the guests and smiling at the appropriate times. She enjoyed the work so much, it wasn't until she started feeling hunger pangs that she noticed April should've been back by now. Speak of the devil…she appeared only a few moments after the thought with a big grin plastered on her face.

"So, did you enjoy your first shift by yourself?"

Rose had a few choice words for April, but then she realized she had enjoyed the shift even though she'd been tricked into it. April took the silence as a yes and continued talking.

"Do you still want to go to the market?"

"That part wasn't a lie as well?"

"No, I'm not that cruel. Shall we be on our way?"

Rose took one look at the empty desk and frowned at April until she pointed at her approaching mother. The older woman looked at them and gave them a shooing motion, and they both left for the market.

CHAPTER 44

Gabriel went to the front desk to find that instead of Rose or the blonde young woman that usually worked at the desk, there was an old woman with platinum hair manning the front. Gabriel approached the desk and said,

"Where are the women that usually work at the desk?"

"My workers are currently making a grocery run. They'll be back on shift in a few hours. Why do you wish to know?"

"I wish to speak to Rose. She's one of your workers and is my traveling companion."

"I see. Well, they'll be back in a few hours, so you may speak to her once they return," the woman said.

He sauntered off to wait for Rose to return.

By the time they'd arrived at the market, the sun had begun to set. It had taken an hour to travel to the market by foot, but it was well worth it. When they got there, Rose was fascinated and overwhelmed by all the different sights, sounds, and smells of the marketplace. The enticingly sweet scent of cinnamon tickled her nose. Fresh eggs were on display, and her mouth watered at the scent of chocolate brownies freshly baked. The smell was heavenly and unfamiliar. Wafting through the air were the scents of various other items she couldn't recognize, but they looked and smelled like meat.

"What is that?" she said pointing to food being served from an opened shell.

"Those are oysters," April said, eyes wide with surprise. "Have you never seen them before?" she asked.

"No, but they look delicious," Rose said, her mouth watering. "I'd like to buy an Oyster Rockefeller," April said, and handed over a few coins in exchange for an oyster topped with shredded greens. The smell reminded her of fish, but it also smelled of salt and vegetables. "Here. I'll take it from your pay," April said with a smile and handed her the food. Rose stared wide-eyed at the food for a moment, before she painstakingly picked out small bites of the food, savoring each morsel. When she took too long, April grabbed her by the arm and tugged her along.

As, they stopped off at a booth with some fresh fruit, Rose asked, "Thank you for the food. So, I've seen your mother at the inn, but I've never seen your father. Does he work somewhere else?" Rose asked.

April's usual cheery gaze turned sad, and she said, "He passed away in a factory accident. My mother inherited the inn from him. It had been his family's business, but he'd never cared for inn work,"

Rose thought about what April had said for a moment, then decided it was best to change the subject. "I'm so sorry to hear about that," Rose feigned distraction at the baked breads and sweets, which wasn't too hard and said, "Look, April, we should get some of those for the inn,"

April laughed and said, "You don't get out much, do you?"

"Not really. My parents were really strict and, up until a few months ago, I wasn't allowed to leave the house much. I mostly worked on the farm and we couldn't afford many sweets. We mostly ate what the farm provided,"she said. She figured that was close enough to the truth. April nodded, and they finished their shopping at the butcher's booth before heading back. The sun had started to set, and they were both laughing and giggling at their own inside jokes.

When they finally made it back to the hotel, it was pitch black. Rose helped April store the groceries and when April told Rose her next shift wasn't until tomorrow morning she decided to head back to her room to get some sleep. Once she made it to her room, she found Gabriel in the doorway with his head in his hands.

CHAPTER 45

While Gabriel had been waiting for Rose, he'd been trying to think of something to say that would make her forgive him, but when he heard her approaching his mind went blank, and he'd frozen in place.

"Why are you here, Gabriel?" Rose said, her voice filled with irritation.

Gabriel tried to muster up the energy to make a snarky comeback, but just sighed in defeat. He knew it would only worsen the situation. He raised his gaze to Rose's, then said, "It's a long story, but if you'll allow me permission to speak with you alone, I'll tell you."

A blush dotted Rose's face for such a brief moment that Gabriel could've imagined it, and she said, "Why should I speak to you?"

"I know what's after you."

"Then I suppose we should speak of this within the confines of my new room?" Rose asked.

"Yes."

"Step aside, so I may open it." Rose waved her hand in a shooing motion.

Gabriel moved out of the way, and Rose fumbled with the lock until it clicked open. Rose walked in, and Gabriel followed after her and then closed the door behind them. Once they were inside the room, Rose whirled on Gabriel and said, "So who is it? Who's after me?"

"It's Nightshade. Another Nymph, but he's darker, evil. He wants Belladonna dead."

Her eyes widened, and she shivered when she heard the name *Nightshade*, "Are you sure that's his name? How do you know it's him?" Rose asked.

"He gave me a *cure* for you. He'd disguised himself as a medicine man. He gave me the potion that ended up being poison. Now, I have to complete a favor for him or else he will kill you and curse me," His body shook, built up anger at Nightshade overflowed and his jaw clenched.

Rose's jaw dropped. Hesitantly she asked, "What is the favor?"

Gabriel sputtered out, "He wants me to kill Belladonna." *I can't believe I told her. What if she hates me*, Gabriel thought. His eyes searched hers for a reaction. She looked shocked, but not angry, and he nearly sighed in relief.

"What are we going to do Gabriel?" She grabbed his arm. Her eyes wide, worried.

"We're going to kill him," he said. His voice was rough, cold.

"If that's the case, I think I know who might be able to help us with that," Rose said.

Rose walked over to where her mirror laid on the ground then picked it up and began saying to it, "Lady Belladonna, we need your help. Please answer your child, Rose."

The surface of the mirror briefly rippled like water in a pond, and when Gabriel walked over to Rose to see what was going on, he saw the face of the woman from the greenhouse looking back at him.

"He's the traitor, Rose! He is the one who made a deal! I saw him in my battle with Nightshade, and he did nothing to help!" the woman shrieked. Her eyes were wild.

"No, my Lady, he wants to help. He's told me that Nightshade will curse him if he doesn't kill you, and he wants to know how we can destroy him," Rose said quickly. The words tumbled from her mouth.

At this, Belladonna paused for a moment, her head quirked to one side in thought.

Then she said, "You cannot destroy him now, while he has his forest, but you may weaken his magic. You must find the source of his power and destroy it. This will weaken Nightshade. Then, we can destroy him."

"But how will we accomplish this?"

"I do not know, my child, but you must do this soon. I sense that he grows stronger by the day."

"We shall do what we can, Lady Belladonna," Gabriel said, and with that the mirror's surface returned to a mere reflection.

CHAPTER 46

That night Rose dreamed about Nightshade.

She was outside her old home. Lady Belladonna and Nightshade stood before her but couldn't see her. She froze to the spot in anticipation of being noticed, but neither of them paid her any mind.

Nightshade was staring into Belladonna's eyes with what looked like affection, but that couldn't be. His pale translucent skin radiated cold, and his hair was so dark that it seemed to suck the light from his surroundings. His teeth were still pointed and bone white. His smile was still devilish, but now he appeared almost handsome, kind. This was not the Nightshade she knew.

Surprisingly, he spoke only kind words rather than harsh ones. *"I give this to you as proof of my devotion. It is a piece of me and only you can destroy it just as only you could destroy my own heart."* His face was sincere, and his eyes were brown and kind. He looked almost human. *"I will cherish it as if it were part of my own heart,"* She said and leaned in to kiss him on the lips. Rose resisted a shudder. Nightshade then presented the mirror to Lady Belladonna. It was the same one that Gabriel had given to Rose.

Rose jolted awake in a cold sweat, and had to take a few deep shuddering breaths. She knew how they were going to weaken Nightshade. But first she would have to go back to her greenhouse. She'd need Belladonna's help. She went to wake Gabriel and tell him of her plan.

FINAL CHAPTER

They had only just made it back to the greenhouse when Rose called out for Belladonna. She held up the mirror and said, "This is the source of his magic. If you look at it closely, you may find it familiar… Mrs. Nightshade."

At that, Belladonna formed before them. She went to snatch the mirror from Rose, but her hand went right through it. Rose realized Belladonna was only half formed.

Then, Nightshade's voice said, "I won't let you destroy me so easily." His putrid tones seemed to curl about her brain, and Belladonna must have heard it too because she stiffened. Smoke curled from the mirror as Nightshade emerged into the human world. Dark smoke coiled around Rose's arm as his body started to form. Gabriel batted uselessly at the partially formed Nymph, his hands sliding through the smoky body.

He fully materialized in the greenhouse, and his presence seemed to take up so much of the space that it made the greenhouse seem like a dollhouse. His hand held a staff made from the bark of the Manchineel tree. Oily black water coiled around the staff. It writhed and coiled like a live beast.

Lady Belladonna yelled for Rose to run away, and then she too formed fully before them in a sprouting of vines. She held a knife formed from plants, it was sturdy like a trunk and the tip dripped with a red sap. Her presence felt brittle and weak by comparison.

She launched herself at Nightshade and caught him off balance long enough for Rose to jerk herself out of Nightshade's grasp.

"Destroy the mirror," Lady Belladonna managed to yell before Nightshade attacked her, and they fell to the ground in a heap.

She launched herself at his throat. Her knife mere inches from his jugular, but he'd blocked it with his staff and pushed her. Belladonna's body shimmered, and her grip loosened on the knife. He moved her back a few inches.

Rose, raving mad, launched herself at the fallen mirror as if possessed by some beast. She punched at it and stomped on it until she was exhausted. Her effort only rewarded her with a small piece of the mirror's glass. It was barely the size of her finger. She grabbed the piece of glass and jabbed at the mirror with it, the only thing fueling her was a maddening need to break Gabriel free from this madman.

Immediately, the mirror started to crack outward from the missing shard. It formed rapidly into small spider webbed cracks.

Nightshade's attention turned from Lady Belladonna to Rose. He pushed Belladonna off of him. His arms twined together in a thicket of thorns and vines. They became sharp as knives and thick as oak. He charged at Rose, trying to plunge his hand into her heart.

Belladonna rushed to Rose and jumped in front of her. Nightshade impaled Belladonna's chest. Belladonna slumped in his arms and lay still, but she never spouted blood, only unraveled into vines that wilted and died as the human form had.

In a blind fury, Rose rushed at Nightshade with a shard of glass in her hand and stabbed him in the chest. He staggered back dazed, as if he'd just been hit by a horse. Rose took that opportunity to dive for the mirror. Her hand still grasped the glass shard as she hit the floor hard. The edges of the glass shard from the middle of the mirror cut her palms as she landed on it. She heard a distinct crack as the mirror broke in half. Nightshade let out a shriek like a wounded animal and Gabriel took that as a cue to body slam into Nightshade's side.

They both went toppling to the ground. Gabriel began to strangle him, desperate to suck all the breath out of Nightshade, until he realized that the Nymph seemed paralyzed.

Gabriel backed up. Rose rushed to his side. Nightshade was mumbling something. It took Rose awhile to realize that it was a question. "Why could you destroy the mirror?"

The thought struck her like a physical blow. If she had destroyed it, then that meant she wasn't only Belladonna's child.

"It is because I, too, am Belladonna. Her magic lives on within me," Rose whispered to the dying Nymph.

At that, he seemed to relax. He made a faint gurgling sound and disappeared into a tendril of black smoke. The dark presence hovering over them had disappeared for now.

Rose fell to the floor and said to Gabriel "It's over. It's done." Tears streamed down her face as Gabriel went to pull her into an embrace.

A faint voice echoed in Rose's head. "No, it's only the beginning, but for now you can rest."

Gabriel pulled Rose tighter to him then said, "When I tried to strangle him I saw the plan flashing through his mind. There are others like him that curse and destroy humanity, and they may come for us now that we have killed their leader."

Rose leaned up and feathered a kiss on his lips. "That may be so, but for now, let us rest and enjoy this freedom from our curses." Gabriel returned the kiss feeling the dark weight finally lifting from his chest.

THE END

Acknowledgments

I want to thank my parents Aileen Wolfe and Steven Goldhirsh for reading my book several times over throughout the writing and editing process and being my first beta readers. I also want to thank my cover artist and mentor, Sukesha Ray, who has helped me with cover designing, event planning for the release, and even social media. Thank you, Jeremy, Raquel, Andrea, Cedric, Vivian, Chelsea, and Josh for being so supportive my first novella. Sergio, thank you for being my extra editor and supporting me at every step along the way, even though you don't read fiction, my physics nerd. I also want to thank my friend CJ, without whom I wouldn't have finished my book in any timely manner. I never would have had the confidence to market my book without my marketing mentor, Stephanie Dolce. Thank you Dinah Miller for your help and support and for being the one to refer me to Annie. Finally, to my amazing editors Charlotte Blowe Stanley and Annie Darek Morgan, thank you for making this novella into something worth reading.